21 Days in October

Magali Favre

21 Days in October

Translated by Arielle Aaronson

Baraka Books

Montréal

Originally published as *21 JOURS EN OCTOBRE*

ISBN 978-1-926824-92-5 pbk; 978-1-926824-98-7 epub; 978-1-926824-99-4 pdf; 978-1-77186-000-0 mobi/kindle

Cover, illustration and design, Lise Rose
Dessin de prison Parthenais, 1970
www.liserose.com
Book design by Folio Infographie
Translated by Arielle Aaronson

Legal Deposit, 4th quarter 2013
Bibliothèque et Archives nationales du Québec
Library and Archives Canada

Published by Baraka Books of Montreal
6977, rue Lacroix
Montréal, Québec H4E 2V4
Telephone: 514 808-8504
info@barakabooks.com
www.barakabooks.com

Printed and bound in Quebec

Baraka Books acknowledges the generous support of its publishing program from the Société de développement des entreprises culturelles du Québec (SODEC) and the Canada Council for the Arts.

We acknowledge the financial support of the Government of Canada, through the National Translation Program for Book Publishing for our translation activities and through the Canada Book Fund (CBF) for our publishing activities.

Trade Distribution & Returns
Canada and the United States
Independent Publishers Group
1-800-888-4741 (IPG1);
orders@ipgbook.com

To Madeleine

Quand on demande à la liberté de montrer ses papiers
à cinq heures du matin [...]
Quand on fait trébucher la Justice
dans les maisons pas chauffées
à cinq heures du matin
Quand la raison d'État se met en marche
à cinq heures du matin [...]

Gérald Godin (1938-1994),
Libertés surveillées, 1975

(Free translation:
When they say YOUR PAPERS to Freedom
at five o'clock in the morning [...]
When Justice gets beaten up
in cold unheated houses
at five o'clock in the morning,
When reasons of state are on the march
at five o'clock in the morning [...])

1

Daybreak

The machines make an awful racket. Wet, fluffy dust clogs his lungs. He coughs and tastes blood in the back of his throat. The pounding of the spinner rings in his head. A warm dampness sticks to his skin.

Finally, the siren sounds. His first week of work is finished. He is replaced by a boy barely older than himself, who expertly checks to see that the threads are taut enough and the barrels of wool are well stocked. The enormous spinner keeps on going, indifferent.

Gaétan crosses the huge room that shakes to the rhythm of fifty machines. He joins the throng of factory workers in the stairwell, their lunchboxes hanging empty off their arms. He goes down three flights and winds up in a line in front of the exit.

He takes his card and slips it into the slot on the time clock. It is 7 a.m. on October 16, 1970. He walks out and the drumming of the machines finally leaves his ears.

The sun is not yet up and the city is bathed in a bluish light. The boy likes this part of the day when everything is still new, when everything still seems possible. He trudges towards Notre-Dame Street, gulping in the fresh dawn air. He exhales, watching his breath condense in the cold air as he waits for the bus. A light frost covers the cars. The last leaves fall from the trees.

The bus is packed, like every morning. The factories along the canal all keep the same shifts, and the old brown buses that heave themselves through the streets struggle to hold the hundreds of workers returning home. Gaétan manages to slip in just before the doors close. He'll be jostled and shoved for nearly an hour, until the corner of Wolfe, where he lives in the *Faubourg à m'lasse* near the port.

He gets drowsy as he leans upright against a pole. His eyelids are heavy; he drifts off. Jerked awake as the bus lurches forward, he sees the steeple of the Notre Dame Basilica through half-opened eyes. Finally, almost there. He can't wait to dive into his bed. But first, he wants to drop by Luc's.

He gets off the bus and walks the length of the giant vacant lot where the new Radio-Canada tower grows bigger each day. He thinks about the endless hockey games he played there with his friends. This part of the neighbourhood that gave way to the wrecking ball has become a vast playground over time. All the boys would meet up there after school; teams were divided by school, always Plessis versus Garneau.

Today fences are blocking the entrance and cranes are already in full swing. Gaétan doesn't have time to hang around anyway, either in the lot or in the lanes. Gone are the days when he'd see his mother up on the balcony hollering that dinner was ready.

Gaétan walks along the never-ending fence. Every day, signs boast new graffiti messages: *FLQ vaincra!* "That was definitely done overnight," the boy says to himself, shrugging his shoulders, before turning onto Rue de la Visitation, where his friend lives. Several years his senior, Luc also works at Dominion—he has been there two years. It's thanks to Luc that Gaétan found the job, though he had to lie about his age.

Two young boys rush past him, schoolbags in hand, and bump into the postman, who continues his rounds as if nothing has happened.

"Let's go, move it along guys! School's begun!" Gaétan shouts at them, laughing.

For the first time, he didn't go back to school this year. At fifteen, he figured that the time had come to push out into the real world. And anyway, his parents need the money that he brings home. In fact, today he got his first pay. Gaétan kicks the ground, sending a big pile of dead leaves flying.

"Now I'm in the big leagues!" he thinks to himself proudly.

He heads down the lane and quickly scrambles up the spiral staircase that leads to the third floor. Pushing through the door, he finds himself in the kitchen, face-to-face with Luc, who still looks half asleep.

"Sorry! I'm too early?"

"S'ok. I have a union meeting before work anyway. So, your first week?"

"It's pretty tough, nights. The noise, the heat... I'm beat."

"No more jerking around at school, eh? Hey, I'll take you for a beer down at the tavern."

"At nine in the morning? If my ma finds out..."

"Relax! It comes with the job. If you can work, you can drink!"

Luc goes back to his room to get dressed. Gaétan admires this determined young man who doesn't take crap from anyone. Luc landed himself a job in shipping at Dominion. He has an easier time of it than the guys in production, even if he has to move boxes all day long. He's not the son of a longshoreman for nothing. He knows the job. "The hardest part," Luc explains, "is dealing with the foreman who's always barking orders in English."

Suddenly, there is a loud pounding at the door.

"Go see who it is!" Luc calls from his room. "I'm coming!"

Gaétan glances through the window of the small sitting room. Two men wearing hats and grey overcoats are standing straight as fence posts on the other side of the door.

"I don't know them, but they sure don't look very happy!"

Before Luc has time to answer, there is a crash of broken glass in the kitchen. Two policemen burst their way through the window and go to open the door for the men still waiting at the front door.

"Luc Maheu?" asks one of them.

"The very one. What are you doing in my house? Is there a problem?"

"We're making the early morning rounds, as you see."

A policeman is already emptying drawers and rifling through closets.

"Do you have a warrant?" asks a stunned Luc, quickly buttoning his shirt.

"My man, I'll have you know that since four this morning we can do what we want. Our honourable members of parliament have been working overtime. Does the War Measures Act mean anything to you? We don't need a warrant now."

"What? But that's not possible!" Gaétan spits furiously.

"You! What's your name?"

The boy lets it go.

"We takin' him too, boss?" asks one of the policemen to the plainclothes cop.

"No! The brats can wait."

Then, turning disdainfully to Gaétan, he says:

"Go back to your parents, or we'll take you with us."

To Luc, he adds:

"Oh yeah, I forgot to tell you that you're under arrest."

"But I didn't do anything!"

"We'll see about that."

The other plainclothes officer takes a pair of handcuffs from his pocket and snaps them on Luc, who is speechless. He pushes Luc towards the door. Gaétan has the presence of mind to hand him a jacket. His friend shoots back:

"Let my ma know, ok? It can't be long, anyway. I haven't done anything. If you can, tell Paul, too. We'll grab that beer next Friday, promise."

Luc is taken down the stairs flanked by the four men and disappears into the police car, like a criminal.

Left alone in the middle of the empty kitchen, Gaétan can't believe what has just happened.

2

Friday, October 16

The boy looks forlornly around the kitchen, now in a shambles. He reaches instinctively for the dustpan and broom, sweeping up the broken glass as best as he can.

"Have to fix the window as soon as possible, or everything will freeze," he thinks to himself. "As it is anyone can get in."

But he knows full well there isn't much to steal here. He dutifully turns off the oil furnace and goes into the bedroom to put the covers back on the bed, above which Luc has tacked a large poster of Robert Charlebois. He closes the drawers, shoving the clothes inside any which way. Then he takes the *Patriote* flag that one of the policemen has torn down and replaces it as it was, hanging it over the window like a curtain.

He has to get out of there, but he's famished and wants to grab a bite to eat from his house before informing anybody. He goes out through the front door that leads right onto Sainte-Rose Street.

Gaétan shivers. Although the sun is up, it is hiding, doing little to warm the air. Mid-October is the in-between season—it's no longer warm, but not very cold either. Too early to bring out the tuques and mittens, but the chill can gnaw right through you.

His red brick house is built right up to the sidewalk. He tugs on the metal lever that causes the bell behind the door to ring sharply. He always wonders how his mother can hear it from all the way back in the kitchen. From the top of the stairs, she pulls the rope that lifts the latch. In a few seconds the door opens. She calls out a tired hello as he climbs up to meet her.

"It's about time! Do you want breakfast or lunch? At this point, you can take your pick. They're already making you do overtime?"

"Nah, I went by Luc's."

"You weren't hanging around the tavern, eh?"

"Come on, Ma, you know me."

"That's just it—I know them, the neighbourhood lot, inside out and backwards. Not even a hair on their chins before they're drinkin' beer."

The boy feels the bitterness in her voice. He wishes she could be proud of him. After all, now that he's working he can help out with the household expenses. But she wanted him to stay in school, to learn English and take a business course. She's told him often enough.

"You'd find a good job with more math and English. You could get out of here, move up the hill. There's nothing but the poor around here, baking in the summer and freezing in the winter in these slums. Drapeau said it: just a lousy neighbourhood that should be torn down. You'd have the chance to get out if you finished school."

Had his mother always been so bitter? No. When he was little, she had been full of smiles and cheer, singing often. But that was before the two younger boys, the demolitions, and especially her husband's accident. Life had ground down her youth, and with it the joy of being a mother.

Gaétan's father had always worked down at the docks. A bad fall five years before had left him with a broken vertebra, putting an end to his days of carrying heavy loads. The company had found him a temporary position in an office, then sacked him. Since then, it had been difficult to make ends meet.

"Here's my first pay," he says, changing the subject. "I'm keeping five bucks."

"I'll finally be able to pay the grocer. So what'll it be, pancake or shepherd's pie?"

"Shepherd's pie."

The boy sits and bolts down his portion in silence. He doesn't want to talk about the morning's events; it might worry his mother.

"I'll have some more."

"Your wages will go to ground beef!" she smiles at him. "You'd better get to bed, rest up from your night of work."

"Nah, I've got things to do."

"What things? You should get some sleep."

"My week's over. Don't worry. Tomorrow I'll sleep all day."

He gets up from the table without waiting for his second helping, takes two slices of white bread and rushes down the stairs.

He feels guilty about leaving his mom standing in the middle of the kitchen. He didn't even say goodbye. But then again, he has his life to live!

Luc is lucky: he might be in jail, but he's no longer under the constant gaze of his mother. Six months earlier, his friend finally moved into the apartment he had spent a year saving up for. He couldn't take living alone with his mother, her watching his every move. One day, not too far in the future, Gaétan hopes, it will be his turn. That's another reason he's started working.

He walks along Dorchester. Four huge cranes stand upright on the other side of the wide boulevard. Three concrete mixer trucks wait in line to fill the wooden formworks. Winter is right around the corner, and the men are working day and night to erect the Radio-Canada tower before all construction stops until spring.

Québec libre! A new slogan decorates the fence. He likes this one. Now that he's working, he understands how Luc's desire to fight for his language is justified. At Dominion, all the workers are French Canadian and all the bosses are English. The French-speaking foremen speak English to the bosses. Real bootlickers, as his father would say.

He's deep in thought when three army jeeps appear in front of him. They race past at full speed, followed by four trucks covered in camouflage. It feels like a war movie; it's the first time in his life that Gaétan has seen such a parade of army vehicles. The convoy passes under the Jacques-Cartier Bridge and turns left on De Lorimier. He can almost see Colonel Vandervoort ahead—Gaétan has always loved John Wayne's character in *The Longest Day.*

He quickens his pace and turns onto Champlain. Then he's facing the steps that lead to the semi-basement apartment where Luc's mother lives.

"Hello, Madame Maheu!" the boy shouts as he walks in, looking as carefree as he can manage.

Her reaction is immediate.

"Where's Luc?"

It's the first time he's been to see her without his friend. She knows instinctively that something is wrong. The radio crackles in the kitchen, announcing a special program. Mme Maheu tries her best to adjust it. Gaétan takes a chair and sits facing Luc's mother, who motions for him to be quiet, forgetting her question. Both pay close attention.

"Around four o'clock this morning, the government took exceptional measures when it announced the implementation of the War Measures Act. Seven battalions of the Canadian military were deployed to Québec to protect both the public and government buildings from terrorist activities. Many searches and arrests are pending. The Premier of Québec will hold a press conference in the afternoon."

Mme Maheu rises to turn off the radio. A heavy silence fills the room. The boy doesn't know where to begin. After a moment, she says:

"It's been on loop for hours now. Reporters are talking about the searches. They're saying the police are stopping anyone and everyone."

Gaétan nods with a sigh, then briefly recounts the arrival of the police and the arrest of his friend.

"The police were just doing what they were told. But why did they arrest Luc? He's not a terrorist!"

When Gaétan admits that he doesn't understand why, anger flashes in Luc's mother's eyes.

As soon as he finishes, she gets up, throws a sweater over her shoulders and heads for the door. Then, she turns back to the boy.

"I'm going to Parthenais. They won't keep my son for long. Coming?"

Gaétan hesitates, surprised by this sudden revolt, but he gets up and follows her. After all, she's right. Luc is innocent. There's been a mistake. They just have to go explain to the police and he'll be let out.

Both walk resolutely up Champlain, then take Ontario to Parthenais Street. Before them rises the massive Sûreté du Québec building, its fifteen floors towering over the neighbourhood houses. It is brand new, huge, and imposing. Halfway up are two floors without windows.

"That's where the prison is," explains Mme Maheu. "The rest is offices."

"It sure takes a lot of pencil-pushers to deal with the bandits," Gaétan says sarcastically.

"It seems like these days they're more interested in the poor than the criminals. I guess they have to get their money's worth and show that it's being put to good use..."

In front of the entrance, a dozen soldiers pace up and down, machine guns in hand.

The neighbourhood kids observe them from across the street, impressed by their combat clothing and weapons. They stand frozen between brazenness and fear.

Luc's mother walks up to the front gate. Two soldiers bar her path with their guns. She explains to them that her son has been arrested. That there's been a mistake. That she wants to see their superior. Nothing works—the soldiers don't budge. Mme Maheu runs out of patience and raises her voice.

"Is my son here? I want to know! You've got no right to keep him!"

The two guards remain impassive. Several policemen leave the building. Gaétan doesn't want the situation to get out of hand. He tugs her by the sleeve.

"Come on, Madame Maheu. We can't do anything here; they won't tell us anything. Let's go."

"I've got a right to know where my son is," she insists.

"No, ma'am," one of the policemen snaps back. "It's the War Measures Act. We can keep whoever we want for as long as the investigation takes. There'll be no contact with the prisoners."

"But my son is innocent."

"Says you. If he was arrested, there's a reason. Now go."

"Where's my son?"

"Ma'am, this is the last time I'm telling you. If I take you inside, it won't be to see your son."

His voice is hard and his gaze unyielding. Madame Maheu can see that all is lost, but she continues to protest.

"Damned mongrels! You heartless bastards!"

The guard is no longer concerned with her. He walks over to the gathering group of children.

"Clear out! Go away! There's nothing to see here."

The soldiers threaten a move towards them, and panicked, the children scatter like a flock of sparrows taking to the air.

The police walk back inside the building. Mme Maheu tries to regain her composure, and Gaétan takes her by the hand.

"Come, I'll walk you back. We can't do anything else here."

The woman says nothing. But her anger growls, waiting to explode at the first turn.

Gaétan thinks of Luc and how the apple didn't fall far from the tree.

It's almost five o'clock in the afternoon when Gaétan finally gets back home. The living room is packed to the rafters—it looks as if the whole neighbourhood has shown up to watch television at the Simards'.

Gaétan's father is fiddling with the notorious rabbit ears he's cobbled together for the TV, trying to chase the static from the screen.

"That's good, Pierre! Don't move!" says one of the neighbours.

"Hey! I'm not staying like this!"

"If you let go, it goes fuzzy."

Finally, his father gently places the antenna on the windowsill. The black and white picture suddenly clears up.

"Bravo, Pop!"

"Be quiet, it's going to start! Shh!"

The screen registers the stiff expression of Robert Bourassa, Premier of Québec. Everyone quiets down.

"Over these past few days, events in Québec have proven beyond a doubt that there must be

limits to exercising our fundamental rights, at least on some occasions, to ensure the normal functioning of democracy.

"I waited until this limit was reached before calling on Ottawa to invoke emergency powers, but just as the risk of anarchy seemed to take on a new dimension, I decided to act quickly and firmly. It was with a heavy heart that I resorted to extraordinary measures. I had no choice. The FLQ is preparing for a massacre, their fourth step in a predetermined plan."

A journalist asks how long the measures will be enforced.

"Naturally, it all depends on the results of the intervention, but I hope that the measures will be as short-lived as possible."

"Unbelievable...our own premier calls up the Canadian army because three nut jobs screwed around. If we get our independence, what then?" his father grumbles.

"Your three nut jobs *did* just kidnap a diplomat and a minister," replies a neighbour.

"A dirty scoundrel working with the mafia."

"Whoa, Pop, you with the FLQ? Careful, or they'll come after you," laughs Gaétan.

"Watch what you say," his mother murmurs, distressed.

The press conference is over, and now they are showing soldiers on duty in front of government buildings.

"That's City Hall! They're scared that we'll come after Drapeau," sneers his father. "They're smart to protect him!"

"I say he should be scared, the bastard! I won't cry for his lot. He destroys our neighbourhood and we're supposed to make nice? At any rate, he won't get my vote, that guy," says another neighbour.

"Kidnapping people, it's ridiculous," mutters his mother.

"And what for? We're just a bunch of cowards. Look at Bourassa, he went crying to Trudeau for help. Can't even take care of his own business himself."

"Pierre, don't be ridiculous! We're talking about two men's lives. Imagine their families."

"And us, our families, when we're out of work and run out of our neighbourhood, who cares then?"

The tension rises and Gaétan knows it'll end badly once again. That's why he doesn't get involved in politics. Gaétan's father has a short fuse and there's always an argument on the other end. Since he lost his job at the port, he blames the whole world.

The room begins to clear out. Gaétan's father and three neighbours decide to move the discussion to the tavern, much to the relief of his wife. The children go back to playing in the lane.

"I'm going to bed," Gaétan tells his mother. "I'm beat."

He's decided not to say anything about Luc's arrest. There's been enough bickering for one day.

3

Saturday, October 17

Gaétan is woken violently by his father's shouting. The two bunk beds are empty. His brothers are nowhere to be seen. He didn't hear them go to bed or get up. It's light outside. He's definitely slept around the clock.

He can hear a nasal voice coming from the television.

The kidnappers could have abducted anyone: you, me, or even a child...

Who is saying such things? The boy pulls on a t-shirt and jeans and makes his way into the living room. His father is already on the couch, a beer resting between his knees.

"Can you believe this? The idiot that's supposed to be governing us decided to frighten everyone. He's saying we might have an uprising on our hands."

Gaétan recognizes Trudeau in the centre of the small screen. In his cold and cutting voice, the Prime Minister of Canada is defending his decision to invoke the War Measures Act.

"Tomorrow, the victim might be a bank manager, a farmer, a child..."

"He doesn't know what he's talking about! The FLQ is going after the politicians, not just anyone."

"You know them, Pop?"

"No, but I know a bunch of guys who're damned worked up. They're frustrated by the lack of progress. Last election, the PQ won hardly any seats compared to the votes they had. It's just like Lévesque said; we're in a madhouse and they're laughing at us. We're sick of always having to go crawling to Ottawa."

Gaétan can't handle his father's tantrums. But the haughty, arrogant, insensitive man who's speaking on the television irks him even more. He has the look of a snake, and Gaétan has no idea where he gets all those well-turned sentences—certainly not from the *Faubourg à m'lasse*.

"Feels good to sleep?" his mother calls from the kitchen. "There's some coffee left, want some?"

Gaétan joins her.

"Yeah, and I'll take some bacon and eggs too. I'm hungry. Are the boys already in the back lane?"

"Yeah, lucky kids. I need some air, too. I can't listen to the news any longer. Your father hasn't moved from his damned TV since the kidnappings. The sooner they find them, the better. This is all just ridiculous."

Gaétan doesn't answer. He doesn't want to get caught in the middle of his parents' argument. Lately there's been an explosion at every turn.

His father has been part of a neighbourhood association since last spring. There have been so many demolitions in the *Faubourg* that it seems the residents are living in a war zone or going through their own Acadian Deportation. Businesses are dropping like flies. Monsieur Pintal's grocery, at the corner of Sainte-Catherine and de la Visitation, is also on the verge of closing. Countless families are having to move. Even Delorimier Stadium, where the neighbourhood used to go watch the Royals play baseball, has been torn down.

His father often recalls how during Expo '67 Mayor Drapeau had billboards put up to hide the slums from the tourists, just waiting to have them destroyed and sell the land off to developers. It's the same old story: the working-class neighbourhoods get no consideration.

"They're ashamed of us!" he says over and over.

Since he's been unemployed, he spends all his time working to bring down the mayor in the upcoming elections, which are to be held in a few days. Now with the recent events, he's always on edge.

But all this energy spent campaigning doesn't put bread on the table. And for Gaétan's mother, times are tough.

"My man does nothing but build castles in the sky," she often sighs.

As soon as he downs his breakfast, Gaétan heads to Luc's mother's house to see if she has heard anything new. A note is stuck to the door: *Luc still isn't home. I'm going back to Parthenais.*

Knowing Mme Maheu, Gaétan has a feeling that she'll be going back every day. Until she has news of her son, they haven't seen the last of her.

The boy walks down Sainte-Catherine, the neighbourhood's most commercial street. The shop windows are decorated with pumpkins, witches, and skeletons stuck to cobwebs. In two weeks, it will be Halloween. Gaétan hasn't worn a costume in two years—he's too old—but he wouldn't miss this night for the world. So he helps his two brothers prepare their costumes and takes them around from door to door. It's Gaétan's favourite holiday of the year. He's already drooling, thinking of the mountain of Kisses he'll devour.

In front of the Beaudry metro station, four soldiers stand guard. "It looks like they've already found their costumes," he says to himself. "Candy will have a funny taste this year."

At the newsstand in front of the metro, the headlines of the *Journal de Montréal* catch his eye: "250 Arrests in One Day!" and "Pauline Julien Jailed Too."

"A singer! They've gone mad!" he thinks.

Until Luc's arrest, Gaétan hadn't paid attention to what was going on. Suddenly, it all seems crazy to him. He had just started working when the first kidnapping occurred—the

British diplomat, James Cross—and he hadn't fully realized what was happening. And since he works nights and sleeps during the day, the opposite of everyone else, he hasn't seen things getting worse.

For the first time in his life, he decides to buy a newspaper.

"Ten cents to try to understand what's going on won't break me."

The CSN building stands at the corner of Saint-Denis and Viger. That's where Paul works, Luc's friend that he was told to warn. But it's Saturday and the receptionist isn't there. Gaétan walks over to the elevator.

A list of the officers is posted, but Gaétan realizes he doesn't even know Paul's last name. At any rate, there is no Paul on the list.

Recently Gaétan ran into Paul at his friend's house. Luc told him that he had met the union leader on a picket line. Paul was distributing leaflets demanding the right to work in French, so Luc got it into his head to switch unions from the FTQ to the CSN. But since it wouldn't be so easy to convince the other workers, Paul asked Luc to come along to the union training sessions to get a better grip on the labour laws.

"It's normal to want to work in your language," Luc often argued.

Two men suddenly walk out of the elevator, whose doors stand open in front of him. He enters without thinking, but where should he go? Which office on what floor? Gaétan turns around and runs after the two men.

"'Scuse me, do you know someone named Paul?"

"There are loads of Pauls, kid."

"I don't know his last name, but he has red hair."

"Ah, that one! I haven't seen him in a couple of weeks."

"I think he's gone to Abitibi to organize some workers," his colleague explains.

Disappointed, Gaétan leaves the building and goes across the street to sit on the steps of the Saint-Sauveur church. He opens his newspaper.

He is so absorbed in his reading that he doesn't notice the young woman who sits down behind him. She cranes her neck to read over his shoulder.

"So, what's your newspaper say?"

Gaétan whips around and blushes when he sees that the girl is so close to him. Big black eyes, short, cropped hair and a cape that swallows her whole. She looks ripped from a picture book.

"Cat got your tongue? Québec's finally moving! You don't think it's too much, do you?"

"Soldiers in the streets and all, does that excite you?"

"That's just to scare us. Me and the other students, we're striking to show our support for the political prisoners."

"Political prisoners?"

"Where have you *been*?"

"I live in the *Faubourg à m'lasse* and I work at Dominion Textile. That ok with you?"

"I didn't mean to give you a hard time!"

"Yeah well, too late!"

Gaétan folds his paper and continues up Saint-Denis.

"She might be cute, but she thinks she's hot stuff," he grumbles to himself, walking.

He turns around at the corner of Sainte-Catherine and Berri, just in time to glimpse a piece of black cape slipping through the door of the metro.

4

Sunday, October 18

Still half asleep, Gaétan pushes open the door of the convenience store. He was barely out of bed when his father sent him to buy a 24-pack. The boy drags his feet, his mind blank.

The radio spits out an aggressive advertisement for Kik Cola. Then comes the news report.

"CKAC reporting, with the latest developments on the kidnappings. The body of Labour Minister Pierre Laporte was discovered yesterday around midnight in the trunk of a car on the Saint-Hubert military base. CKAC received an anonymous call in the evening revealing that a statement had been left in the lobby of the Port-Royal Room in Montréal's Place des Arts. Our reporter Michel Saint-Louis was sent to the area and found the statement confirming the execution of the minister and indicating the place where his body could be

found. The document was immediately delivered to the Sûreté du Québec. At precisely 11:45 p.m., Sûreté explosives experts opened the trunk of a green Chevrolet. A body identified as Laporte was found inside. The car had been abandoned on the Saint-Hubert military base, on the South Shore. A special program honouring Minister Pierre Laporte will follow this report. Stay tuned to CKAC, your number one news station."

Behind his counter, Mr. Pintal, the owner of the grocery store, remains unruffled, surrounded by the colourful boxes of penny candy. He's already had time to digest the news: the report has been running all night.

A group of dishevelled youths enters the store rowdily, one of them carrying a stack of leaflets. He hands one to the grocer and puts the others on the counter. Mr. Pintal is shaken from his silence.

"Take that garbage off my counter. You've come to the wrong place."

"You support the War Measures Act? A government that denies democracy? Mass arrests? You don't support freedom of expression?"

"That's enough! Get out of here, you rotten kids. I'll have you know that I don't support people who murder ministers."

The young man doesn't argue the point, and the group leaves to hand out their leaflets elsewhere. Gaétan watches them walk away through the window. They slip their papers in each mailbox along Rue de la Visitation.

The boy discreetly picks up a leaflet that has fallen on the floor. It advertises a public meeting Monday evening at the Cégep du Vieux-Montréal theatre. While he reads, the old radio starts broadcasting a special report:

"In the interest of public information for our listeners, CKAC has decided to broadcast the content of the statement found last night at Place des Arts: 'In light of the arrogance of the federal government and its servant Bourassa and due to their blatant hypocrisy, the FLQ decided to take action. Pierre Laporte, Minister of Unemployment and Assimilation, was executed at 6:16 this evening by the Dieppe cell (Royal 22nd). You will find the body in the trunk of a green Chevrolet (9J-2420) at the Saint-Hubert military base. We shall overcome! FLQ.'

"The authors of the statement added a postscript, declaring 'Those who exploit the people of Québec had better watch out.'

"To clarify, we wish to point out that the authorities still have no word about Mr. James Richard Cross, the kidnapped British diplomat."

Still red with anger, Mr. Pintal gives Gaétan his change.

"At least you work. You're not like those snot-nosed students who let their hair and beards grow long. A bunch of bums, trying to tell us what to do! They support terrorists, they want a revolution. Luckily the police and the army are doing their job. I'd send them all to jail, if it was up to me!"

The boy takes the case of beer with both hands and leaves without a word.

Suddenly, doubt creeps into his mind. Could Luc, his best friend, be mixed up in this business? Why did the police arrest him? He thinks back to the rare political discussions they had together. Luc, outraged by the exploitation of French Canadian workers, had explained why an independent Québec was so important.

Gaétan racks his memory for a clue that might connect his friend to the FLQ. But he doesn't find any. Luc is just a victim of the many arbitrary arrests. "If they're arresting singers, they wouldn't stop at a factory worker," the boy tries to reason.

Gaétan deposits the case at his father's feet.

"Here are some reserves, Pop! Hear what they did?"

His father shoots him a dirty look.

"It's barbaric," he continues.

"Talk to me when you've had thirty years in the factory behind you and they give you the boot."

"That's no excuse!"

"No, but it's an explanation."

"But kidnapping people doesn't make sense!"

As Gaétan turns to leave the room, his father holds him back.

"Stay!"

Looking his son right in his eyes, he speaks to him in a strangely calm voice.

"You know, I have a different way of taking care of you than your mother. I've felt rebellion creeping all through me ever since I haven't been able to feed my family right. I'm not heartless, you know. But when you're forced to swallow your pride and scrimp and scrape the bottom of the barrel to get by, it gets to you. I've had odd jobs. What I want is a real job. I'm a worker, not a beggar. So I fight my way through. When I see you heading to the factory, following in my footsteps, it hurts. I don't know what'll come next. To me, a guy planting bombs is just a guy who's been workin' in the shop for twenty years and who's just been given the boot. He's just had enough!"

He stops. Gaétan is speechless. It's the first time his father has spoken to him like this. For the past two days, the boy has been feeling as if he's being forced to grow up too quickly. His childhood is disappearing, and he's not too sure where that leaves him.

Gaétan runs into his mother as he leaves the house to head to the factory. She has just come from the courthouse, where the body of Pierre Laporte is exposed in the chapel. She's brought along his brothers.

"It was so moving! Me and the kids prayed for the poor man. He didn't deserve that. I hope the little ones will learn a lesson. Violence brings nothing but tragedy. Like Trudeau said, the FLQ is a cancer we must destroy."

Gaétan feels like a slice of baloney stuck between two pieces of bread. And it's getting more and more uncomfortable.

5

Monday, October 19

A large grey-stone building towers over Sherbrooke Street. Gaétan hangs back before entering. This place doesn't feel like it is meant for someone like him, someone who never even finished high school. The building he walks into every day is red brick with big chimneys.

He is still holding the leaflet that he picked up from the grocery store. He has decided to get a closer look at the wild-haired students who have been flocking in greater numbers to his neighbourhood.

A group of young people arrive. They all look like the gang of toughs at the grocery store. They speak loudly and wave their arms. Gaétan follows the crowd towards the room where the meeting is being held. It's already packed. All of the comfortable red-velvet seats are already occupied. Some people sit on the floor in front of the stage, others remain standing, spilling out into the aisles. Even the balconies with the wrought-iron railings are jammed. Gaétan takes a moment to admire his surroundings. There are big, ornate iron girders supporting the ceiling. A thick red curtain frames the stage where the speakers are seated, looking over their speeches behind a table. Behind them hangs a faded backdrop of an exotic landscape, no doubt left there from the last student performance. The room is noisy, with plumes of smoke rising to the ceiling.

The first speaker stands and a hush falls over the crowd.

"Friends, we're making history. Unprecedented events have been unfolding before our eyes for some time. Kidnappings, politically motivated assassinations, mass arrests, the army's invasion of our city..."

A unanimous cry of protest makes its way around the room.

"We, the students of the Cégep du Vieux-Montréal, must decide how to best respond to these events. To make an informed decision, we have invited various political players to come speak. Unfortunately, several of our guests weren't able to make it today because they were arrested last Friday at dawn..."

Another cry of protest goes up. Many students shake their fists in the air.

"I want you to know that nearly a hundred Québec students in Paris decided to occupy Canada House in order to show their support for the FLQ manifesto and denounce the state of emergency called for by the War Measures Act. Our struggle has now gone international..."

But Gaétan is no longer listening. He has just glimpsed a large black cape hidden among a group at the back of the room. Without thinking, he edges his way closer.

It's her all right, the girl he met Saturday on the church steps. She stands out from the crowd with her short hair and enormous earrings. She still hasn't noticed him, and he sneaks glances at her from a distance. She listens to the speeches attentively, nodding in agreement or shaking her head in disapproval, alternately applauding or booing the speaker. Her eyes sparkle.

Gaétan wants to approach her, but he can sense that it's not the right time. The speaker ends his speech to thunderous applause.

"Vive le Québec libre!"

"Le Québec aux Québécois!"

"Le FLQ vaincra!"

At these last words, the crowd's single focus is shattered. Some begin to chant the FLQ slogan while others whistle. Many stand up to show their disapproval. There are shouts:

"We can't support murderers!"

It's complete chaos.

A young man with curly hair takes the stage and tries to restore the calm.

"I'd just like to explain the position the Parti Québécois has taken regarding these tragic events."

"Collaborator!"

"Be quiet, he's got the right to speak! This is a democracy!"

"Independence!"

Microphone in hand, he walks towards the front of the stage and begins to speak. Little by little, the crowd calms down.

Gaétan approves of his moderate remarks, reminding the audience that René Lévesque publicly condemned all acts of violence during his latest press conference. He attacked those responsible for the cold, deliberate execution of Mr. Laporte, an act that has sullied the reputation of all Quebecers.

The crowd quiets down; all ears turn attentively towards the speaker. The respected politician's words seem to reach the audience. He concludes:

"Never let the cause, whatever it be, lead to murder, so long as we are free to move forward democratically."

An ovation. The crowd is unanimous once again. Gaétan applauds wildly. He shoots a glance over at the girl, who doesn't seem to quite share his enthusiasm. Her eyes sweep the crowd, and she meets his gaze. She stares at him for a moment. He gives a small wave with his hand.

She flashes a magnificent smile.

"Louise, look who's here," says one of her friends, taking her arm.

She turns and throws herself into the arms of the young man who has just arrived. They seem happy to see each other.

Gaétan looks at his watch, slightly disappointed.

"I'd better leave anyway if I want to make it to the shop on time," he says to himself. "I've heard enough."

As he makes his way out, he thinks that at least now he knows her name. She must study here, but did she recognize him? Something tells him the answer is yes.

He finds himself alone in the cold. It's dark. It takes all his courage to walk down Sanguinet to the Berri-de-Montigny station. The metro seems sinister tonight.

6

Tuesday, October 20

"Have you gone back over there?" Mme Maheu asks him.

"No, not since they took him in," Gaétan answers, surprised by the question.

"Last night, I wanted to go clean up his apartment but I saw some lights on," she says. "I didn't dare go up. At first, I thought he'd come back. But there were two of 'em, a guy and a girl. I didn't want it to look like I was a snoop, so I left right away."

"That's strange... Who could be living at Luc's?" Gaétan wonders.

Every day after his shift, the boy stops by to see Mme Maheu and ask about his friend. But she still hasn't heard anything, despite all the time she spends outside of Parthenais.

"The man I saw was shorter and stockier than Luc. And he was smokin' a pipe. Who d'you think he could be? I'm worried. Do you know if Luc has a girlfriend?"

"I don't think so."

Gaétan can sense the concern in his friend's mother's voice, but he also detects a bit of curiosity. Mme Maheu had a difficult time accepting her son's departure and is always eager to learn more about his life away from her. But the more questions she asks, the less he answers.

All the same, all this talk of unknown visitors intrigues Gaétan.

"I'll pass by tonight to see if there's still someone there."

"You're real helpful, thank you. You never know, maybe it's just some rubby crashing in an empty apartment. In any case, I'll be waiting to hear from you. I'm going to the Laviolette Baths, do you want to walk partway with me?"

"Ok."

Since Luc moved out and left Mme Maheu alone, she has a hard time filling up her days. When she has company, she doesn't let it go easily. She recounts her life story, explaining how she raised her son all on her own. It's her greatest source of pride.

Because he knows all of her stories by heart, Luc can't stand listening to her go on and on. But this is all new to Gaétan. He listens attentively, thinking she has a gift for storytelling, and she enjoys it.

"You know, Gaétan, I can't believe that Luc's done anything wrong. He was always a good boy. I brought him up right, even if he never knew his father. Poor man, there was an accident unloading a ship—a crate fell on 'im, killed 'im. I didn't even know I was pregnant. We were to get married in the spring."

Gaétan has known this for a while, but he lets her continue.

"We didn't have it easy at the end of each month. But even when I didn't have a cent to my name, I had my tricks. Luc never lacked anything. When a shipment of molasses arrived at the port, I used to get up early and go down Notre-Dame to the reservoirs. I lived on Panet back then, but now it's all been demolished. It was a long walk to Frontenac. I'd bring lotsa small containers, we all did. You had to come at the right time and sneak through the fence to the dock. When they were finished unloading, the crane operator would drop a barrel, like it was an accident. All us women would rush to fill our containers. You had to do it quickly, because they kept an eye on those docks. We weren't supposed to be there. Sometimes we returned empty-handed 'cause the operator had forgotten us. Or maybe he was being watched. We never found out who it was, but that man put a smile on so many young faces in the neighbourhood."

They arrive in front of the Laviolette Baths on De Lorimier, where Mme Maheu comes once a week to wash since she doesn't have a bathroom. The boy leaves her, promising to return with a full report the next day.

But Gaétan wants to get to the bottom of it right away. He goes directly to Luc's and rings the doorbell. No answer. He looks through the door pane: everything is quiet.

He decides to go through the back lane. He carefully peeks through the kitchen windows. The apartment is empty. He enters.

The remnants of a breakfast are lying on the kitchen counter. The bed is unmade. Yet he had cleaned up before leaving on Friday. The furnace is on. He leaves without touching anything. Mme Maheu wasn't making it up. Someone has definitely spent the night here, and it appears that whoever it is will return. Gaétan decides to come back in the evening to find out more.

A few hours later, he's back. An icy drizzle makes him shiver. It's dark. "What a terrible night to play James Bond," he mutters to himself.

From down in the lane, he can see a light coming from Luc's apartment. He climbs furtively up the spiral staircase and sneaks onto the porch. He's stunned by what he sees inside.

A tall redhead is cooking: it's Paul, Luc's friend from the union. Paralyzed by his discovery, Gaétan remains crouched in the shadows.

Paul sets the table, and a young woman whom Gaétan doesn't recognize comes over to join him. She wears a terrycloth bathrobe with a towel wrapped around her head. She has clearly just gotten out of the bath. They sit down to eat.

"They're making themselves right at home!" Gaétan murmurs, surprised.

The couple is listening to the radio as they eat their spaghetti. Through the open window, Gaétan can hear the report of Pierre Laporte's funeral, which had taken place that afternoon. The funeral music drowns out what is being said at the table.

Clips of newspaper articles are strewn about the counter. On a scrap of paper the boy can see a sketch of a *Patriote* with his hat, pipe, and gun. It's the same one that he saw yesterday on television, on the FLQ manifesto.

"FLQ members. And they're hiding out at Luc's."

Gaétan remembers Robert Bourassa's every word, explaining at a press conference that they would press charges against anyone aiding members of the FLQ.

Does Luc know what's going on in his house?

7

Wednesday, October 21

"I can't wait for the first snowstorm. At least it'll really be winter," thinks Gaétan as he walks through the morning fog.

Each year, the period between the last leaves falling and the first snowfall seems endless. He hates this time between seasons. With the weather, as with life, it's better to just pick a side. At the moment, his thoughts are wavering as much as the thermometer.

Throughout his shift, he couldn't shake the image of the *Patriote* that he saw on Luc's table last night. Gaétan is torn between wanting to know and being afraid of what he might find out. Should he head back to Luc's for an explanation from Paul or go warn Mme Maheu?

When he manages to forget about this for a moment, an image of Louise pops into his head. Her smile is etched in his mind, confusing him even further.

He finally decides to go home and get some rest, putting off any decisions for the moment.

"I might see things more clearly after a few hours of sleep," he tries to convince himself.

He walks home with the resolute air of someone who has solved a difficult problem. The apartment is empty and silent: no radio coming from the kitchen, no television in the living room. Neither his father nor his mother is there. Not stopping to wonder why, he heads blissfully to his room.

He's about to slip between the sheets when the doorbell rings. He goes to open it, grumbling, and finds himself face to face with Mme Maheu.

"You never came to see me, so I came to get the news."

Gaétan feels caught with his pants down.

"Hang on, I'm coming!"

The last thing he wants is for his parents to run into her if they happen to come home soon. He throws on some clothes with a weary sigh, thinking of his bed, and pulls the door closed behind him.

"We'll go to your place. Sorry, I'm just so beat, I wanted to sleep a little before coming to see you."

Gaétan tries to buy himself some time, not knowing if he should tell her the truth.

"I made you some muffins and coffee." She seems annoyed.

Gaétan feels sheepish. Why is he always trying to help people? After all, it never ends, and it always comes back to bite you!

Sitting in front of a steaming cup of coffee, his mouth full with a delicious raisin bran muffin, he finally explains what he saw at Luc's. He tells her what he knows about Paul, but is careful not to mention the young woman.

"He's a friend of Luc's, a union guy who works for the CSN unions. Luc wants to change Dominion's affiliation. He thinks the American unions don't do enough to help French Canadians. Their representatives don't even speak French. They don't understand our problems. Paul told him he could help."

To his surprise, Mme Maheu nods her approval.

"And he's right. I stopped working because of that. I worked in English all my life and nearly cracked afterwards. I was an accountant for a small company that made bike parts. I prepared the payslips. We were mostly French Canadians, a couple of Italians. And everything was in English! It's not right to spend your whole life in English working for peanuts. By the end, I was even dreaming in English. I would have nightmares where I couldn't speak at all. I just kept mumbling things half in English, half in French. It was awful; I was so mixed up. When Luc was old enough to work, I gave it all up. I prefer to live poor but speak my own language. I haven't spoken a single word of English since, and I won't speak another damned word until I die. I spoke enough at work."

Dumbfounded, Gaétan listens to her attentively. He can see that when it comes to this topic, both mother and son agree.

"Maybe Paul needs somewhere to sleep," she concludes, "and Luc gave him permission to stay at his place. We shouldn't worry if it's a friend."

As he walks away, Gaétan thinks Mme Maheu is smart to trust her son. They shouldn't be getting involved.

The icy mist has cleared and the sun is shining in a cloudless sky. Gaétan no longer wants to go back to bed. He decides to take a walk. He climbs the Cartier hill and heads into Parc La Fontaine. He gulps in the smell of wet fallen leaves and grass. There are patches of ice here and there. A squirrel approaches him, begging for crumbs. But his pockets are empty.

This time of year, his father usually goes out hunting. Last year, Gaétan went with him for the first time. He even had to miss a few days of school.

"Hunting is the best school," his father had said, justifying his absence.

But this year, with all that's going on, he didn't even bring up the possibility. Gaétan would have gladly gone back, though. His father is a good hunter, and he almost always brings back a deer. He's never missed a season before; this is the first year.

He usually goes with his friends from the port. They all save their holiday weeks for the fall. The trip out to the woods with his old work buddies is always sacred.

Last fall, Gaétan had gone up north with them. They'd driven five hours in a clunker that was so old that, from where he was sitting on the backseat, the boy could see the road whizzing by under his feet.

After bumping over dirt roads through La Vérendrye park, they had finally reached a lake. There, a round wood cabin was waiting for them.

"Here, we live like woodsmen. Like descendants of the *coureurs des bois* who discovered America and walked all across the continent. Here, we can get away from the city, our women, our bosses, and the English. I give you paradise!" his father had declared upon arrival.

The boy would never forget those hours spent in the icy cold of the early morning, eagerly awaiting a flash of deer antlers through the black spruce. He could never forget the silence of the night buzzing with a thousand rustles and whispers that had filled his head with imaginary beasts.

It was also during this trip that he had tasted his first Molson, had experienced his first hangover. His father had kept the rite of passage secret.

The last night they'd made a huge campfire down by the lake to cook pork and beans. They had buried the cast iron pot in the sand, in the fire's ashes. The next day, they were ready for breakfast. The best pork and beans he had ever eaten. Just thinking about it made his mouth water.

And of course his father had brought back a deer, tied to the roof of the car. A trophy that, like every year, attracted the admiration of the whole street.

That unforgettable week had been one of the rare times Gaétan had left the city.

His forest was Parc La Fontaine more often than not. He liked to walk around, especially during this time of the year when the park wasn't crowded. The ducks had been put away for the winter, the *Jardin des Merveilles* was closed, and the squirrels had made themselves scarce. Only the eternal pigeons were left. They were indestructible; not even the coldest weather bothered them.

But since he's seen the real forest, the park seems sparse. Just a sad little garden to someone who's experienced the wild and boundless forest of the North.

Gaétan leaves the park, glum.

Over by the library, a bunch of young men with scruffy beards sit on the steps, smoking and talking loudly.

Gaétan thinks about Louise.

8

Thursday, October 22

"You buy the newspaper now?"

His mother hands him his plate, eyebrows raised. Her son isn't going to get into politics now too, is he?

Gaétan devours his peanut butter toast while reading an article in the *Journal de Montréal* with a catchy title: "There Will Be Blood If Montréal Elects the FRAP."

Another article reports that Jean Marchand, the federal minister, stated in a Vancouver interview that the FRAP or *Front d'action politique* is just a front for the FLQ.

Gaétan pushes the newspaper away, sick of these outrageous comments. Just because the FRAP is made up of trade unionists and working-class citizens doesn't mean it's linked to the FLQ. He and the politicians clearly don't live in the same world. Elections for a new mayor are in three days, and it seems that they're going to stop at nothing to scare the public.

"It's disgusting!"

"You sound like your father."

"Well he's right—Drapeau's destroying our neighbourhood. He's angry because he's out of work. Being resentful doesn't make him a terrorist."

His mother looks at him, bewildered. It's the first time that Gaétan has stuck up for his father. She sits down heavily on her chair. She has always tried to protect him from her husband's ideas.

"You're going to end up like him!"

"So what? Pop's still fighting. He could just as easily drown his life away in his beer and spend his days at the tavern, like the rest of them."

"It's always the same damned thing. Those guys think they're such hot stuff, and then we have to pick up the pieces. It's a waste of time."

Gaétan gets up with a start, knocking over his chair, and leaves the room. He's had enough of his mother's whining. He needs some fresh air.

Gaétan has a few hours to kill before returning to work. He wants to use them to take his mind off things.

He finds himself in front of the Cégep du Vieux-Montréal. Classes are back in session, and he can see students walking in and out of the building. He watches their comings and goings from across Sherbrooke Street. Three students, their arms full of leaflets, sit down outside the main entrance. A girl wearing a black cape comes to join them. Gaétan has trouble admitting that she's the one he's been waiting for.

He crosses the street and pretends to walk in like any other student. She hands him a leaflet and he takes it without hesitation. Suddenly, she recognizes him.

"I thought you worked at the factory."

"I work nights."

"That can't be easy! You left so quickly, the other day."

Gaétan glances at the paper. He can't really understand the words on the page: working class, capitalism, imperialism, revolution… it's all gibberish to him.

Louise reacts to his sceptical expression.

"I can explain."

"It's ok, I know how to read!"

"That's not what I meant."

Clearly, they have a hard time understanding each other. She suggests they grab a coffee together inside.

"The guys can finish handing them out without me. Coming?"

Gaétan, still wary, accepts. He's curious to know more about this strange girl. He follows her in.

"This is our spot," she says, proudly indicating a small room lined with posters.

A banner hangs against the back wall: *Continuons le combat! Contre les mesures de guerre! Québec libre!*

Piles of leaflets are heaped on desks, nearly covering several textbooks. A Gestetner duplicating machine sits on a desk next to a typewriter.

"Is this how you study at Cégep?"

"It's not just the classes that count. We have to pay attention to politics when we learn, too. You're not one of Trudeau's federalists, I hope?"

The boy looks at her mocking face, and wonders who she thinks she is, a student explaining to the layperson just what is good for him? As if there weren't enough priests already.

He'd like to give her a piece of his mind, but thinks better of it. Now isn't the time, if he wants to grab that coffee with her.

She keeps talking, using the same words that were in the leaflet. He watches her closely, but he isn't really listening. She's making no sense, speaking in a different language, but she's so pretty in her fit of passion that he doesn't say anything. He'd even be willing to agree with her to keep hearing her talk. Gaétan's silence encourages the girl.

Suddenly, the three boys barge into the room for more leaflets.

"Are you coming, Louise?"

"One second, I'm finishing up explaining what we're doing."

"Lucky guy, getting private lessons!" one of them says sarcastically to Gaétan. "If he's bothering you, I can take over, Louise."

"It's ok, Jacques. He's not from Cégep."

"Where's he from? Not a spy, I hope," says the second boy. "We need to be ready for anything from the police right now. You know that the administration'll ban our group at the slightest provocation."

Louise shrugs.

"You're paranoid! I told him to come. He works at Dominion Textile."

Gaétan is uneasy being the centre of attention and wonders if he should just leave as soon as possible.

The third boy, who has turned on the radio and is listening to the news, calls for their attention.

"Hey, guys! The three big unions have come together to call for the War Measures Act to be revoked. They condemn the FLQ's actions, but they're calling for all people being arbitrarily detained to be released."

"Yeah! Bravo! Great!"

Gaétan's thoughts go immediately to Luc, hoping he'll be released soon. He gets up.

"I have to go."

"Wait up, I'll walk with you."

Louise seems relieved to leave the room and find herself alone with him.

"Are you coming back tomorrow?"

"I don't think so," he replies, feeling like he doesn't belong here among all these students.

"Tomorrow's Friday, and I have the afternoon off. Come meet me, we can go for a walk. Do you know the Chat Noir? It's a café not far from here, on Sherbrooke. I'll be there at one. Come by if you want."

"Maybe..."

9

Friday, October 23

Today, the temperature has fallen below zero. The sun is shining and the sky is a bright blue. There isn't a drop of moisture in the air. The horizon is sharp, as if carved out by a knife. But the city spreading from underneath Gaétan's feet isn't the one that he knows.

Of course he can recognize Dominion's chimneys off in the distance, dominating Saint-Henri, further still is the river, and on the horizon he can see the mountains of the Eastern Townships. But to get to where he is standing, he has crossed through a part of the city he never knew existed.

Gaétan couldn't wait to see Louise again. After his shift and a few short hours of sleep, he went to meet her at the Chat Noir, where she was waiting. It was early afternoon and the café was almost empty. She was sitting alone tucked away in a corner, her nose buried in a thick book with a green cover. When he arrived, she placed the book on the table and he could read the title: *Les nègres blancs d'Amérique (White Niggers of America).*

"What are white niggers?"

"It's you and me; it's all of us! Here, French Canadians always have the worst jobs. We live in the most miserable neighbourhoods, and the bosses are always English."

"You need a book to tell you that? I bet you're just another revolutionary!"

Louise ignored his remark and changed the subject.

"Do you want to go see the bird park?"

"Where's that? I've never heard of it."

"It's in Westmount."

"I've never been to that part of the city."

"There's a park up there that no one knows about. Well… almost. The view of Montréal is incredible. It's a nice change from the top of Mount Royal. It's just behind Saint Joseph's Oratory."

"I know that one. My old Aunt Rose used to take us there; she wanted to show all the kids Brother André's heart. I've even seen people going up the steps on their knees. We'd already seen everything by the time they got to the top."

The young pair had taken the 144 Bus on Avenue des Pins, skirting the base of Mount Royal. They had passed by rich-looking houses. One of them had caught their attention; a battalion of soldiers was standing guard in front of it.

"Some bigwig must live there," Gaétan remarked.

"No kidding: that's the Prime Minister's house."

"Boubou?"

"No, not Robert Bourassa. The other one, the big decision-maker, Pierre Elliott Trudeau."

"The guy who threw Luc in jail?"

"Who's Luc?"

Gaétan spent the rest of the trip detailing his friend's arrest and how worried he was.

"Listen, some of my friends are defending the political prisoners. Maybe they could get you some information."

"Luc, a political prisoner?"

"No, but maybe they could at least be able to tell you where he's locked up. And maybe get in touch with him."

They got off at the corner of Cedar Avenue.

"Here all the street names are in English. We're in Westmount," Louise explained.

"Geez, the English are hiding up in the hills! They don't want us to see their money and wonder where they're getting it from?"

"You're going to see places you didn't even know existed."

Leaning against the lookout's cement wall, Gaétan admires a house below: an immense building with a greenish copper roof is joined to a tower and a large veranda that serves as a greenhouse. The yard is framed by a stone wall protecting the lush, green garden. Below, a gleaming Jaguar waits patiently in front of a two-door garage.

"Three or four families from the *Faubourg à m'lasse* could fit into that castle. All my neighbours have to come see this. What a house!"

They take a small path that leads towards the centre of the park. The trees are bare and the wet earth smells like dead leaves.

Everything is still; there isn't a person in sight. In the middle of a small clearing, a bench underneath a beautiful bare maple tree seems to call to them.

From here, they can no longer hear the heartbeat of the city. Here, they forget everything from the factory's siren to the soldiers on patrol and the arrests at five in the morning. It's only them and the birds.

"WHAT'S YOUR NAME?"

Louise and Gaétan jump with surprise and whirl around. Two policemen, whom they didn't see approach, repeat the question in English.

"What is your name?"

"I'm Louise, and this is Gaétan," she answers in French.

"Where do you live?"

"We're not from here," Louise answers. "We live at the bottom of the mountain, further down."

"They don't speak French?" Gaétan asks naively.

"This is Westmount. You cannot loiter here. This park is restricted to residents. For security reasons."

"What are they saying? They can't speak French like everyone else?" he grumbles.

"They're saying that we can't stay here. The park is reserved for residents only."

"Please, you must leave!"

"Nature isn't for everyone?"

Gaétan lets out a low *"Fuck!"* under his breath, the only English word that he knows.

"Please, return to your district."

Not having a choice, they get up. One policeman leads the way and the other follows them, escorting them to the park's exit.

It's the first time that Gaétan has been thrown out of a place like this, and he can't believe it. But he keeps a lid on his anger, unlike Louise, who is visibly upset.

"You'd think we were in a South African township or on an Indian reserve. Better not step on their stupid grass with our shoes covered in poverty and filth. 'Cause it's so civilized here an' all!" she exclaims, putting on a working-class accent.

"Watch it, you!" the smaller of the two policemen, a redhead, barks roughly at her in French with a strong English accent. "I'm from down the mountain."

"It's funny how they understand us when we raise our voices!"

"That one must be one of the Irish from Verdun," Gaétan snorts.

"He's from the British side, the strongest side!" Louise adds scathingly.

When they get to the end of the path they leave the park, relieved but furious.

10

Saturday, October 24

Y flottait dans son pantalon
De là lui venait son surnom
Bozo-les-culottes
Y'avait qu'une cinquième année
Y savait à peine compter
Bozo-les-culottes
Comme il baragouinait l'anglais
Comme gardien de nuit il travaillait
Bozo-les-culottes
Même s'il était un peu dingue
Y'avait compris qu'faut être bilingue
Bozo-les-culottes

Raymond Lévesque, *Bozo-les-culottes, 1967**

---

* Free translation: *"His trousers a bloody shame/ It's where he got his name/ Bozo-in-Britches/ Never learned to hold a pen/ Could hardly count to ten/ Bozo-in-Britches/ In English he'd jabber away/ Worked all night and slept all day/ Bozo-in-Britches/ Though he barely went to school/ He knew that English was a handy tool/ Bozo-in-Britches."*

For the first time in his life, Gaétan understands the song that Luc used to play on the patched-up turntable he had rescued from the street. He'd never really paid attention to the words before. But they sunk in yesterday in that neighbourhood full of hypocrites. He had felt the conqueror's deep contempt of his language when the police officers spoke to him in English. Gaétan recognizes the working-class man who had never held a pen: it's his father.

Pauline Julien's passionate voice seems to nearly explode the small transistor perched on the kitchen shelf.

CKAC has just announced the singer's release from prison. At the end of the song, the announcer explains that despite her release, police officers have raided her house again and arrested her fifteen-year-old son, eighteen-year-old daughter, and the cook.

"They're all crazy!" Gaétan exclaims.

"Don't forget that the police are still looking for James Cross," his mother replies. "I heard those terrorists have enough explosives to blow up the whole city. The mayor said they're looking to seize power."

"But Pauline Julien is a singer, not a terrorist."

"Yes, but she's spreading her bad ideas to the public. Doesn't she talk about dynamite in her song?"

"Don't be ridiculous! You should stop listening to Frenchie Jarraud's gossip on CKVL. That's all just to scare us. The Parti Québécois and even Claude Ryan, publisher of *Le Devoir,* is calling for the municipal elections to be postponed because of all the insane rumours going around. And they aren't extremists."

"Either way, it's because of the stupid FLQ bums that the army is everywhere."

Gaétan sighs. There's no point arguing with his mother.

"You got two cents, Ma? I want to make a call."

"Who to?" she asks, smiling.

"Someone's curious!"

She tosses him a coin, laughing.

"A mother can try! At your age, you should be paying more attention to girls than to your father's crazy ideas."

Gaétan slips on his coat and runs to the phone booth on the corner. Bell cut off their phone service two months ago because of late payments. With his next paycheque, the family might get the phone line back.

It rings several times. No answer. But Louise had told him that she'd be there this morning. He walks back home a bit disappointed. He'll call back later.

Instead of going into the house to listen to his mother grumble, Gaétan decides to pass by Luc's to see if someone is still in the apartment. He hasn't been there since Tuesday.

As usual, he takes the back lane, which looks forlorn at this time of year with its empty clotheslines. Gaétan likes to see all the colourful clothes flapping in the wind. It makes the neighbourhood seem festive. He sneaks around some children who are playing street hockey. Two large cardboard boxes serve as goals. Each Saturday morning, the lanes are alive with the shrieks of children pretending to be Jean Béliveau or Yvan Cournoyer. Tonight, they'll all be sitting in front of their televisions to watch the Canadiens play the Philadelphia Flyers.

When he gets to Luc's balcony, Gaétan notices that the door pane has been replaced. He looks through the window. Everything is in order. Is Paul still living here? He goes in and walks around the apartment. There isn't a trace of him anywhere. He's disappeared.

Although he has no news of her son, he heads over to see Luc's mother and tell her that Paul is no longer in the apartment.

"I heard on the radio that the people who were arrested without warrants are beginning to be released," he tells her. "Luc should be getting out soon."

"I dunno. There are new raids and new arrests every day."

Gaétan doesn't reply. He doesn't tell her about the drawing of the *Patriote* he saw lying on the counter or that Paul is supposed to be in Abitibi. He doesn't want to worry her.

"You staying to eat? I made a *tourtière*."

Gaétan doesn't dare say no—and anyway, there's no turning down Mme Maheu's *tourtière*. She gets out a jar of homemade pickles. He bites into a tangy pickle, all crunchy and delicious.

In Mme Maheu's house, as in all the other neighbourhood houses, the radio is constantly crackling in the background. When they hear the theme song to the news, both listen attentively.

"The Montréal police have just announced that a message from the FLQ has been found. Its authors demand the immediate release of union leader

Michel Chartrand, lawyer Robert Lemieux, and Patriotes Pierre Vallières and Charles Gagnon, or Montréal will pay."

The woman and the young man look at each other, bewildered. The announcer adds that the police are questioning the document's authenticity.

"And with the elections tomorrow," Gaétan sighs. "It's not looking good!"

11

Sunday, October 25

Louise still isn't answering her telephone. There's been no sign of her since Friday. Gaétan walks around in circles in the empty apartment. What a strange Sunday. It's the day of Montréal's municipal elections. His father is an official at a polling station; he'll be there all day. His mother left with his little brothers to go vote and then take a walk up Mount Royal. Gaétan has no doubt of her support for Mayor Drapeau.

Gaétan is restless. He sits down in front of the television but doesn't turn it on. On Sunday afternoons there is never anything to watch. Instead, he watches the movie that is playing in his head. It seems as if he's just lived through the past week in fast-forward motion. As if he isn't quite the same person who, a week earlier, had casually ridden the bus to the factory for the first time. Is life really all about working for wages that are spent in a flash? He thinks of Louise studying, of his father selling his soul to put food on the table, of Luc languishing in prison.

"And where do I fit in all of this?" he wonders.

He is overwhelmed by a wave of helplessness. Fortunately, the ring of the doorbell pulls him from his thoughts. He jumps off his chair and bounds down the stairs, opening the door. In front of him stands a police officer.

"Mme Simard, please."

"She's not here."

"Who are you?"

"Her son."

"Ok. Well tell her that she can come pick up her husband at the station."

"At the station? What's the matter?"

"I'm not at liberty to say. Pass the message on to your mother. Tell her to come by before eight o'clock, or he'll spend the night in station 22."

The police officer hands him a ticket. He can barely make out the words scrawled on the page: obstruction of justice and injury to a police officer.

By the time he looks up, the police car is already gone.

Gaétan walks back up the stairs and lets himself drop onto the sofa.

"Should have expected that from Pop! He can never keep quiet. Looks like he's jealous of all the others who were arrested for no reason," grumbles the boy.

He's now tied to the house: he has to wait for his mother to come home to tell her the news. Even if Louise were back he couldn't go see her.

After cursing his father, he decides to turn on the television in order to pass the time. A man and a woman are standing on a small bridge, talking. The actors have a funny accent and use expressions that he's never heard of. In the background he can make out the name of a run-down hotel: *Hôtel du Nord*.

Apparently the French don't all speak like schoolmarms. These two must come from the *Faubourg à m'lasse* of Paris, he reasons.

Gaétan is sleeping on the sofa when Richard and Patrick, his two brothers, jump on top of him. Their hands are like ice and their cheeks are rosy.

His mother is already in the kitchen making hot chocolate for everyone. Gaétan gets up and runs after his brothers, pummelling them good-naturedly. The two younger boys scamper into the kitchen where they run rings around the table before ending up hiding behind their mother's skirts.

"Scaredy cats! Scaredy cats!" Gaétan taunts them, happy to be surrounded by family.

"Get out from there, you little rascals! And go sit down, I'm about to pour the hot chocolate. Careful, it's boiling hot!"

Everyone immediately grabs a seat around the table. With almost religious silence, the three boys bury their noses in their mugs.

"I'm gonna get supper ready. Your father should be home soon."

Gaétan almost chokes on his last sip. He gets up and goes to find the ticket he left lying on the sofa.

"Here. The police came and gave me this earlier. You have to go get him at the station."

"Goddammit! He couldn't just keep his mouth shut, could he? I don't have time to go before you have to leave for your shift. I'm not leaving the children all alone."

"I could maybe stay and watch them."

"There's no way you're missing work because of your father's antics. I'll go tomorrow morning when the boys are at school. Anyway, a night in there might set him straight."

12

Monday, October 26

"Drapeau re-elected with 92% of the vote."

On the front page of the newspaper, the headlines are relentless. The opposition hasn't won a single seat. The fear campaign orchestrated by the two governments as well as by the mayor himself worked like a charm.

Gaétan doesn't want to go home this morning. The mood in the house must be unbearable. After a night spent in jail, coupled with the election results, his father is surely in a foul mood. Once he has left the factory he calls Louise, who finally picks up and invites him to come by her house.

He walks along Cherrier looking for number 928. There it is: a big grey-stone house with ornate wooden doors. He climbs the steps leading up to the porch, but hangs back a moment before ringing the doorbell. A real doctor's house, as his mother would say. The door opens, and a young man wearing ripped jeans and an army jacket comes out, brushing past him.

"'Scuse, man!" says the tall bearded man, leaving the door wide open behind him.

Gaétan throws a curious glance inside.

Before him, there's a long hallway that leads to a dining room. The floor is waxed. Gaétan takes off his boots so as not to get it dirty. On each side of the hallway, doors open onto rooms lined with posters of celebrities, the mattresses resting square on the ground. There are newspapers and magazines strewn everywhere. He sees a guitar in one corner, a djembe in another, a turntable hidden underneath a stack of LPs, clothes thrown about haphazardly. Complete chaos!

An old wooden table fills up the entire dining room. The remnants of breakfast are still scattered everywhere. A number of plants sit on the windowsill overlooking a small backyard. On the wall, someone has painted *Flower Power* in broad strokes, surrounded by peace signs and small bright flowers. Louise comes out from the kitchen, still wearing pyjamas, coffee in hand.

"I'm sorry... Someone let me in," stammers the boy, uncomfortable that he has surprised her this early.

"Do you want some coffee?" she replies, not in the least unsettled by his presence.

"Sure, thanks. You don't live with your parents?"

She goes back into the kitchen, where he follows.

"My parents are in Magog, in the Eastern Townships. I wanted to study art at the Cégep du Vieux-Montréal. They finally agreed to let me go, as long as I live with my brother. That's where I was this weekend, at their place. I forgot to tell you."

"How many of you live here?"

"In the double room there's my brother and his girlfriend. I'm in the room behind the kitchen. And there's two guys in each of the other two rooms. All together, our rent is cheap. And it's more fun than being alone in your own apartment. Here's your coffee."

"I don't know if I'd like living with so many other people," says Gaétan, thinking that if he wanted to move out it would be so that things would quiet down.

"No one asked you to move in," Louise answers curtly. "Come on, we'll go in my room."

The boy feels that he should have kept his mouth shut. Again. He follows her.

The mattress is covered with a duvet and many colourful pillows. A bookshelf mounted on bricks covers the length of one wall. The shelves sag dangerously under the weight of the books. In one corner, a barn door supported by wooden frames serves as a desk. On the wall are posters of Jimi Hendrix and Janis Joplin. Between the two, on a large sheet of white paper running from floor to ceiling, a poem has been recopied by hand. The title, *Speak White,* written in red, looks like a bloodstain.

"Does your brother study, too?"

"Yeah, at Université du Québec."

"And what do the other guys do?"

"Nothing!"

"They don't work?"

"No, they don't want to participate in consumerism. They refuse to become either the exploited or the exploiters."

"But then how do they have enough money to live?"

"They live on love and fresh air," she answers in a mocking voice. "They're hippies. But their father has a lot of money. That helps."

"Well I don't have the choice not to go work. My mother needs my paycheque to make ends meet. I don't know how I could do that."

"It's not the same thing. You're a factory worker."

"Anyway, I don't know what I'd do if I didn't work. Seen this?"

Gaétan hands *Le Journal de Montréal* to the girl.

"You see what terrorism does? In early October, the opposition was at thirty percent. Today, it's evaporated."

"That's what you came to tell me? The governments would have found some way to eliminate the opposition anyway."

"We don't have to feed their fire."

An awkward silence follows. The boy has been there barely fifteen minutes and already they have a hard time understanding each other. He is beginning to wonder why he continues to see this girl.

"You know this record?"

Louise pulls an album from under a pile of papers on the desk. She wants to lighten the mood.

"Listen to it while I get dressed. I just bought it."

She places the vinyl on the turntable, delicately drops the needle onto the outer edge, and leaves.

A woman's voice, quiet and mournful, fills the room. She sings of a black eagle rising into the night. The tension and crescendo of her voice, both deep and fragile, trouble Gaétan.

Louise returns just as the song is ending. She has put on a long pastel-coloured Indian dress and large earrings. A huge smile lights up her face. "In the end," Gaétan thinks, "it was a good idea to stay." This girl is beautiful, full of life, and she has introduced him to a world far from the *Faubourg à m'lasse*.

They sit on the bed and chat for a while. Then she tells him that she has class at eleven o'clock.

"You can stay if you want."

"I don't want to bother anyone."

"You're not bothering anyone. You can keep listening to music."

The offer is tempting, and Gaétan accepts. He doesn't have the strength to go back home. And he feels so good here.

Once Louise leaves, the boy digs greedily through the stack of records. He's never seen so many! He stumbles upon *Québec Love* by Charlebois; he recognizes this one.

He sits down on the bed, lulled by the rhythm of the first track.

Suddenly, light is blinding him. Louise is standing in the door frame.

"You're still here!"

Outside, it's dark. Gaétan panics.

"What time is it?"

"Nine at night."

"I fell asleep and I didn't see the time passing. I gotta get out of here, or I'll be late for work."

Dazed, Gaétan gets up and splashes some cold water on his face to wake up. Louise brings him his coat and, laughing, says, "You're my Cinderella! Wait, give me your phone number."

"I don't have a phone. I'll call you tomorrow. See you!"

As he runs to the Sherbrooke metro station, he realizes that he hasn't eaten anything all day. He doesn't even have a lunch with him. It's going to be a long night at the shop.

13

Tuesday, October 27

"Where'd you sleep last night?"

He is barely in the door when the unavoidable question hits him.

"I'm starving! Can I get some bacon and eggs?" Gaétan responds, ignoring it.

"You're not getting anything until you tell me what you were thinking, not calling last night. I was worried to death. Your father's still in prison, you know?"

"Why's that? You were supposed to go pick him up yesterday morning."

"If you'd a'come home last night, you'd know that the police decided to keep him a while longer. They wouldn't even lemme see him, and I don't know when he'll get out."

Gaétan should have known that with his father, nothing would be simple. Feeling sheepish to have abandoned his mother at such a time, he tries to explain.

"I went to see some friends and I fell asleep. When I woke up, it was too late to come by the house."

The boy is purposely vague. The plural allows him to avoid specifying—without lying—that he had slept in a girl's room. If his mother knew, she would hit the roof.

"Gaétan, you're the oldest and you know I count on you when your father isn't around. Don't ever do that again!"

It hits him like a ton of bricks. He wants to hand over his wages to his mother to help make ends meet, but taking care of his brothers is a different story ... yet he knows that when you come from the poor side of town, you can't afford to spend the day in bed listening to music. Reality washes over him, and he realizes just how serious things are.

"Listen, I'm sorry about yesterday, but I had no way of knowing ... I know someone who has some contacts with lawyers," the boy continues, trying to calm his mother down. "I can talk to them."

"You of all people know that we don't have a penny to spare for things like that."

"I know, but they can do it for free when you're in a tight spot like us."

"Promises are a dime a dozen! Eat your eggs, and until your father gets back, try to spend more time around the house."

That evening, Louise and Gaétan walk down the church steps to the basement of Saint-Louis-de-France. The room is full, and there is hardly a pause between speeches. Louise explains that this is the first meeting of the Prisoner Support Committee. She grabs Gaétan's hand and they weave through the crowd to a table where they are asked to sign a petition demanding the release of the political prisoners.

Gaétan recognizes the young man Louise had been so happy to see at the Cégep assembly.

"This is my brother, Mathieu. He studies law. Tell him about your dad, maybe he can do something."

Gaétan recounts the circumstances of his father's arrest. He also describes his father's stubborn and rebellious personality. He had probably hurled a volley of insults at the police during his arrest, which no doubt explains why they've kept him so long.

"Write down his name, address, and where he was arrested. Explain the circumstances of his arrest in a few sentences."

"I also have a buddy I haven't heard from since October 16. He was arrested at his home at dawn. Could you do anything for him, too?"

"Name, address, and circumstances. Write all that down," answers Mathieu, handing him a sheet of paper.

Gaétan looks helplessly at Louise. She immediately recognizes his predicament and takes the paper from her brother.

"Go ahead, tell me. I'll write."

Gaétan gives her a warm smile. He's always had to struggle to write more than three words without making a mistake. She's getting him out of a tight spot.

While Louise finishes taking down Gaétan's information, the boy glances around at the assembly.

He listens to the speaker, who is denouncing the harsh government measures. But his mind wanders, reminding him of his school days. As the teacher explained cross-multiplication, his head would be filled with thoughts about the upcoming hockey game. Back then, the blackboard would be covered in meaningless symbols. Today, the words are reduced to simple background noise.

Louise finishes writing and hands the sheet to her brother. She stays near the table to help others sign the petition. Gaétan decides to wander a bit.

Suddenly, he recognizes a face several metres away. Paul! With his red beard, he is unmistakable.

Gaétan inches closer, but can't bring himself to address him. This older man intimidates him. He is standing, broad-shouldered and straight as an arrow, listening carefully to the speeches.

According to what Luc has told him, Paul grew up in Ville Jacques-Cartier, a particularly poor area of the South Shore, where he had fallen into the life of a bum.

"It's easy to find money if you've got guts," he had told Luc. "You buy a gun and rob the first bank you see. Where I come from, you've got a choice: either you become a bum or you work yourself to death for peanuts. But my days as a bum didn't last long."

What made him change his ways wasn't so much the fear of ending up in jail as it was the idea of making it on his own. He couldn't accept the notion of having money and living the good life while watching others suffer. Making money itself isn't that difficult but wanting to change one's ways is another story. He wanted to make sure there were no more Ville Jacques-Cartiers a few kilometres away from the Town of Mount Royals. That's why he became a union leader.

"I started fighting to get us some sidewalks in Ville Jacques-Cartier," he had told Luc, laughing.

"But what does he really do today?" Gaétan wonders. "Maybe he's up to his old tricks?"

"What's your problem? Why are you staring at me?" The man's tone is cutting.

"You don't recognize me? I'm Gaétan," stammers the boy. "We met once or twice at Luc's."

"Oh yeah, I remember. You were going to start working at Dominion." Framed by thick eyebrows, his gaze is both driven and warm.

"Exactly. I was wondering if you knew that Luc's been arrested," the boy replies.

"No, I didn't. With everything going on, I haven't seen him for a while," admits the man, visibly irritated by the boy's presence. He throws anxious glances around the room.

He doesn't seem to appreciate that he's been recognized. With a tight smile, he cuts the discussion short. "Look, I'm sorry, but I gotta go."

Without further explanation, Paul slips into the crowd and heads towards the exit. Intrigued, Gaétan falls in step behind him. Once out on the street, the man walks towards the Sherbrooke metro station. Without hesitation, Gaétan passes unnoticed through the turnstile after him. A train arrives. Paul jumps into one of the cars. Gaétan gets on the next one.

The metro pulls out of the station. It's incredibly hot. Gaétan discreetly watches Paul, who is reading the newspaper and trying hard to look relaxed. The stations fly by and the boy remains alert. At the Sauvé station Paul rises quickly, like someone who has forgotten he has reached his stop, and steps onto the platform just before the doors close. Gaétan doesn't have time to react and he watches, powerless, as the man disappears.

His surveillance was short-lived. He's been had. He thought vaguely that if he discovered where Paul lived he would learn more about him. Now he's come up empty-handed, realizing to boot that he's ditched Louise without an explanation.

At the Henri-Bourassa station, he changes direction and takes the metro back towards the assembly. The speeches are over. Few people remain in the room, and Louise is gone. He searches in vain for a familiar face. Discarded pamphlets mixed with cigarette butts litter the floor. The room has the stale feeling of a party that's just ended.

14

Wednesday, October 28

"What'd you do, go AWOL?"

"What do you mean?"

Gaétan is shivering inside the phone booth. He called Louise as soon as his shift was over, despite the early hour.

"It's a figure of speech. You've got nothing to say to me?"

"I'm sorry about last night, but something came up."

"You ran into a pretty girl?"

"Don't be ridiculous! I'll explain tonight. I need to see you. It's important."

"I have a lot of work today. I need to study every once in a while, you know. And I have a paper due on Louis Riel. It's fascinating!"

Gaétan can feel that his disappearance last night has hurt her. How can he regain her trust? Then, he has a sudden idea.

"Louis Riel! My father used to tell me about him."

"So?"

"My great-grandfather knew him."

"Is that a joke?"

"No, it's true. He went out West as a settler."

"Come by the Chat Noir tomorrow night and you can tell me all about it."

"Alright. See you!"

"And rest up so you're in shape. Expect an interrogation."

Gaétan hangs up. His hands are blocks of ice, but he's just won a small victory. Now that he's sure to see Louise again, the boy hurries directly home. He promised his mother he would be there to take care of his brothers.

The two boys, just back from school, jump on his bed to wake him up. Gaétan looks at them through half-opened eyes. The sun is already beginning to fade away. These days, it seems that the sun is always angry with him. Gaétan goes to bed and it's barely light out. He gets up and it's already dark.

"Mama said you have to take care of us," says the younger boy.

Gaétan pulls himself wearily out of bed and drags his feet into the kitchen. As long as he's home he would have liked to sleep a little more. But he did promise.

"You guys want toast with peanut butter?"

"No, cookies from the box!"

Gaétan smiles. "The box" is the red metal container where his mother puts her famous cookies—oatmeal, molasses, or gingerbread, depending on what she feels like making or what's left in the kitchen cupboards. All the children on the block have tasted them. At Christmas, she uses it to store her fruitcake, which can stay there for a month. Even empty, the box smells spicy enough to tempt a saint.

"Want a glass of milk, too?"

"Can we watch TV?"

"Go ahead, I'll bring everything in."

Deep down, Gaétan is proud to be taking care of his brothers, to be responsible enough to say yes or no. He enjoys preparing their snack, which he puts on a tray and brings into the living room.

"Wow, what service! Thanks!"

"I'm giving you a treat today, but don't think it's gonna be like this every day. After *Fanfreluche*, go do your homework," he says in a voice he wants to sound authoritative.

"We don't even got any!"

"I doubt that. If I remember correctly, Mme Paquette gave homework every night. Don't even try to pull a fast one on me."

"I just have a little math to do," admits Patrick.

"I got some grammar exercises," Richard adds. "You gonna help us?"

"We'll see. In the meantime, move over! I want to watch *Fanfreluche*, too."

The two boys jump aside to make a place for him in the centre of the sofa. The show's theme song begins and Fanfreluche appears, opening her enormous book. Today, the mischievous doll with her pigtails pointing in all directions is going to the circus, where Mme Dora will predict her future. As usual, when Fanfreluche doesn't agree with the story, she jumps into the adventure to change the ending.

Gaétan prefers *Sol and Gobelet*, the two clowns who always get themselves into crazy situations. But they're on Tuesdays. And anyway, the boy doesn't want to deny himself this pleasure. A good snack in front of a children's show is always a special treat.

The boys have just opened their notebooks on the kitchen table to start their homework when their father's voice rings out.

"Man alive! It's good to be back home!"

The whole family comes to surround him.

His wife, who has come in with him, smiles broadly when she sees the notebooks on the table. She hugs Gaétan and thanks him for taking care of his brothers.

"You might not be so happy when you see that the cookie box is empty."

"I'll make more. You can see they didn't keep him too long. I bet they'd had enough of him!"

"It's unbelievable, arresting people like that!" exclaims Gaétan's father.

Before his son's sceptical gaze, he recounts the events surrounding his arrest while Gaétan's mother begins preparing the evening meal.

"I wanted to make sure people weren't cheating at the polls. I was positive that the big guy with the brown hair wasn't Mr. Gosselin. I've seen Mr. Gosselin before, thought he was a little tubby guy, an' what's more, he died last spring. I said as much to the election officer, but he didn't wanna hear it. I got mad and they had to call the police to come take me outta there."

Gaétan smiles, imagining the heap of abuse the police must have taken.

"Laugh if you want, but I know I was right. So I'm being charged for insulting police officers. I gotta appear in court in a month. You call that justice, arresting the guy who saw someone cheating and letting the cheater off the hook? Those damned cops, can't find the guys setting off bombs and kidnapping a minister, but they sure can give us regular folks a hard time!"

"Spaghetti's ready! Time to eat!"

They all gather around as the mother fills their plates, happy to be together again.

15

Thursday, October 29

He pushes the café door open. A thick cloud of smoke envelops him. Charlebois' *La Marche du président* is playing softly. In every corner, the young and the old with their long hair and scruffy beards are smoking and drinking, talking loudly and lustily. A little unnerved, Gaétan sweeps the room with his eyes. Eventually he can make out a shadow with short hair, the shortest of the room, boys and girls combined. Louise is bent over a notebook, surrounded by several volumes. He sits down in front of her, his eyes already red from the smoke.

"How can you work in this place?"

"I feel less alone than in my room. I like it. So, what happened to you the other day?"

Since waking up that morning, Gaétan has been searching for a way to avoid telling her about Paul. But he can't lie.

"I have a friend who has a friend..."

"What?"

He has to start from the beginning. As he moves through the explanation, Louise is listening to him with increasing attention and maybe even a hint of admiration. At the end of his story, she exclaims, "Wow! I didn't know you hung around with guys in the FLQ!"

"It's not what you think—and don't talk so loud! Luc's been my friend since forever. He's a good worker. He only wants to improve the conditions on the job, and Paul offered to help him. I don't really know him. But Luc's not a 'revolutionary' like you say, let alone a member of the FLQ. He knows that killing a minister won't ever make things better."

"Obviously if we do nothing, we don't risk a thing!"

"But when we do too much, we give our enemies the ammunition they need to scare everyone."

"And you say you don't understand politics at all."

"Factory workers can understand things, too. My father's an active member of a citizens' committee to get rid of Mayor Drapeau, who's been wreaking havoc on our neighbourhood for years. And now a bunch of bums who think they're better than everyone come and screw everything up."

"Speaking of your father, I bet you were just messing with me when you said that your great-grandfather knew Louis Riel."

"Not at all!"

Gaétan begins to tell her the family legend, carefully handed down over the past three generations.

His great-grandfather's name was Lionel Simard. He had only one leg, and when you asked he'd tell you how he lost the other one in a battle against the English. It was his pride and joy.

He had begun to work in Montréal at a young age, as a day hand for the Masson family. There he'd met a young man from the immense prairies that stretch as far as the eye can see on the other side of the Great Lakes. His name was Louis Riel. He studied at the Collège de Montréal's Petit Séminaire and had only one desire: to return to the banks of the Red River. Lionel listened for hours as Louis described the immensity of the region's fertile land and the miraculous buffalo hunts. In his mind, this wild, bountiful nature was meant to be shared among all people of good will. So when Louis Riel returned to his lands, Gaétan's great-grandfather, then only seventeen, didn't think twice before going with him.

Lionel cleared a plot of land that ran like a strip up from the Red River and a long way into the land behind. He built a camp with help from Louis Riel and his Métis friends. The families were very close-knit. Whenever one of them went through a difficult spell, they all helped each other. Life there was rough, and without the knowledge picked up from the Indians, few would have survived. Lionel managed one wheat harvest, but the following year everything was destroyed by locusts. Luckily, there was hunting, fishing, and the fur trade with the highest bidder winning, be it the American or the British companies. So they managed to survive, even when crops failed.

But the Canadian government at the time had strong views on how the region would be developed, since it had just been bought from the Hudson Bay Company. And the Métis had no place there.

When government surveyors came to divide up the land English-style, as if no one had ever lived there, the Métis banded together to prevent them from completing their paperwork. Louis Riel became their leader and formed a temporary government. Lionel was wounded during a battle with the English settlers who had come from Ontario to settle on land he had cleared himself. He was wounded in the leg and it had to be amputated. For him, it was the end of a dream. He came back to Montréal, never to set foot on the Prairies again. As family legend goes, Lionel Simard, the tough, uncompromising man who had managed to raise a family of twelve children on only one leg, had cried the day they hung Louis Riel.

"I even think my father still has a picture of Lionel in front of his camp on the Red River."

"You've got to show me! I'll make a photocopy and put it in with my paper," says Louise.

Gaétan can't believe that an old family story he's never paid much attention to fascinates the girl. He watches her earnestly write down his story in her notebook, savouring being the object of her interest.

16

Friday, October 30

It's three o'clock in the morning. Gaétan takes his place next to the spinner with a heavy heart. At the end of the large machine room where the noise is deafening, a shabby little room with a few picnic tables and a vending machine invites the workers to have a bite to eat during their breaks.

As he does every night, Gaétan goes in to gulp down two bottles of Coke to keep his eyes open until the end of his shift.

Today, a woman who could have been his mother was crying in a corner. She had just been fired for missing a few days of work because one of her children had been sick. When she returned, she had already been replaced by a younger girl. The foreman hadn't even warned her. She had tried to negotiate another position, even one less well paid, but it was no use.

Now, the roar of the machines scrambles his thoughts. Gaétan can't get the woman's expression out of his head. He would have liked to help her. He has a sudden desire to drop everything, to run away from this place where life seems to count for so little. He remembers Luc's words: *"Cheap labour. All we are is cheap labour."*

A nagging question runs through his head. How many years will he spend in front of this machine? Thirty? Forty? He is sick to his stomach.

Suddenly, his machine gets caught and a few of the threads snap. It's a catastrophe. He pushes the red emergency button and the foreman comes running.

"Goddammit... Better not let that happen too often, or believe me you won't stay here long. It takes three hours to get that machine going again—that's three hours' production time lost."

Gaétan says nothing.

"You can get the hell out of here for today. In three hours, your shift'll be over. But I'm holding a half-day on your paycheque."

Gaétan turns and bolts towards the stairs.

"You heartless bastards!" he yells behind him. Fortunately, his voice is covered by the noise of the machines.

Gaétan finds himself outside under a starry sky. At this time of night, it is more than just cold. Neither the buses nor the metro are running. He will have to walk back across the entire city. Tonight is a night full of anger. Gaétan clenches his fists.

He is now trudging down Sainte-Catherine. Usually so full of life and light, it is strangely deserted. Tomorrow is Halloween, and the store windows decorated with skeletons, ghosts, and witches end up giving off a gloomy feeling. There are hardly any cars; only a few taxis circulate, looking for the last stragglers after a night on the town.

The boy arrives at the corner of the Main. It's the only place in the whole city where snack bars are still open at this late hour. Boulevard Saint-Laurent, its real name, is the stomping grounds of prostitutes and other non-conformists of all types. Gaétan decides to go eat a hot dog at the Montréal Pool Room before going home. A woman beckons to him from the door of a nightclub. He quickens his pace.

Once he has bolted down the hot dog, he continues walking, quickly crossing the area where his mother doesn't like to see him hanging around. For her, the Red Light district is where the mafia made their fortune during American prohibition. And if she still supports Mayor Drapeau, it's mainly for his crusade against these visible remnants of those dissolute days.

Gaétan gradually leaves the lights on the Main for the dark and familiar streets of his neighbourhood in the East.

Two vagrants are sleeping under an air vent outside of the Beaudry metro station. They are wrapped in old sleeping bags and surrounded by several empty liquor bottles, a symbol of their daily struggles.

Gaétan has definitely seen his share of misery tonight.

To avoid explaining the reason for his early return, he decides to spend the rest of the night at Luc's. At the same time, he'll check to see if the apartment is still empty.

It's garbage day, and the lane is overflowing with garbage cans. A rat, eagerly sniffing the contents of a ripped bag, scurries away as Gaétan approaches, only to return right after he passes.

Exhausted, Gaétan climbs the stairs and enters the apartment. He walks through all the rooms; the apartment is empty. Nothing seems to have moved since his last visit. His legs have gone numb. Without thinking, he collapses on Luc's bed and pulls the blankets around him. He falls asleep instantly.

"Get up! Get up!"

Gaétan is being shaken vigorously. A flashlight beam is shining in his eyes. Blinded and dazed, he can't see the person who is roughing him up. What does he want?

"Hey! Stop shaking me!"

"Who're you? Where's Paul? Hey! Answer!"

"Jesus! Let me go!"

"It's ok, he's awake. Let him get up."

Gaétan sits up, stunned. He can make out three shadows in front of him. It's still dark outside. He glances at the clock: four in the morning. He's only been sleeping for an hour.

He's dizzy and disoriented. The only thing he wants is to go back to sleep.

"Leave me alone. I don't know what you're talking about."

"Get up. Follow us into the kitchen. We have some questions to ask you."

As he speaks, the man switches on the overhead light. Blinded, Gaétan closes his eyes and then opens them again slowly. He's stunned. At the end of the bed, three police officers are staring at him.

17

Saturday, October 31

It's been twenty-four hours!

Gaétan is sitting in a corner of his white-walled cell. Alone.

LWM23.

Left wing, mezzanine, cell 23.

He never, ever would have imagined he'd end up in the Parthenais jail. Why did he decide to go sleep at Luc's? It's two weeks later, almost to the hour, and now he's in the same predicament as his friend.

And he'd promised his brothers he'd spend Halloween with them ... He's always loved trick-or-treating! Patrick is going as a cowboy and Richard as Zorro. On top of everything, he'd invited Louise to join them. What would she think when he didn't show up at the Chat Noir? He'll be standing her up again.

The silence surrounding Gaétan is strange. He almost misses his brothers' shouts and the racket of the factory. This silence is broken only by the slamming and creaking of metal doors.

When he got to Parthenais, a police officer took fingerprints of his five fingers. Then Gaétan had been searched, finding himself stark naked in front of a stranger for the first time in his life. An impassive guard asked him to spread his legs and bend over. The boy did as he was told, biting his lips until they bled from humiliation. He couldn't believe that he was being treated like a criminal. The guard handed him his prison uniform: a brown shirt, grey pants, and boots, all too big for him.

Immediately afterwards, he had been interrogated by two police officers in a small office harshly lit with a neon light. One of them typed out his responses with two fingers.

"Family name?"

"Simard."

"First name?"

"Gaétan."

"Address?"

"1307 rue Sainte-Rose, Montréal."

"Occupation?"

"Spinner at Dominion Textile."

"Nationality?"

"French Canadian. No, *Québécois*!"

"Don't be a smart ass," replied the officer.

Gaétan was scared stiff, sitting up straight on the metal chair facing these two men who were looking him over head to toe with all their arrogance.

He had told them the truth. But that hadn't been enough for them. They had decided to let him mull things over in a cell, confident that his memory would return and that they would get what they wanted.

Was he a member of the FLQ? What did he think of all the political violence? Did he know a certain Francis Simard or a Jacques Rose?

The questions seemed utterly ridiculous to him. He kept repeating that he had seen those names for the first time in the newspaper a few days earlier, that there was no family connection to Francis Simard, that he was just a factory worker at Dominion Textile.

On the wall above the desk, next to a map of Montréal, a poster with four headshots read: *$150,000 reward for any information leading to the arrest of Francis Simard, Paul Rose, Jacques Rose, Marc Carbonneau.*

Just like in the westerns!

Alone in his cell, he has time to rehash everything. He thinks about his great-grandfather. He thinks about the mansions in Westmount. He thinks about his father, about Louise, about the others being held in here like him, for no reason. Maybe Luc is in one of these cells, not far from him. But he doesn't dare call out.

A squeaky trolley makes its way over to his cell. A guard, flanked by two officers, opens the door and hands him his lunch.

"I'll come by to pick it up in twenty minutes," he says, almost mechanically.

Gaétan takes the tin plate. There are four slight depressions to hold food. The sauce spills over onto everything; the bread is soaked, and the jello swims in the water from the beans that haven't been properly drained. The boy sets his tray down on the ground, disgusted, and goes back to sitting in his corner.

A guard drags his keys against the cell doors, a noisy way to announce his arrival and annoy the prisoners. His footsteps approach. To Gaétan, it seems that the jailer enjoys prolonging the prisoners' agony. Everyone is wondering which door he will stop at. And when someone is brought in, it's never clear if it's for an interrogation or for release.

This time, it's his turn.

"Let's go!"

As always, the guard is flanked by two officers. The small troop walks down the corridor in silence. Gaétan glances furtively into each of the cells, hoping to recognize Luc, who must be somewhere in this building.

A metal door opens onto a small room, identical to the one where he had his first interrogation. Gaétan's stomach drops.

"Family name? First name?"

"Here we go again," thinks the boy, trying his best to answer their questions regardless.

"What were you doing at Luc's house?"

Gaétan can't hold back a smirk.

"I was sleeping."

"Why didn't you go back to your own house? Were you planning on meeting someone?"

"I just wanted to sleep in peace. I didn't want my parents asking me questions."

"What kinds of questions? About your terrorist activities?"

"That's ridiculous! I already told you, I'm just a factory worker at Dominion. I dropped out of school and I need my paycheque. I'm not crazy."

"Watch it! We've been keeping our eye on Luc Maheu's apartment for the past week. We're concerned with the comings and goings of a suspect named Paul Dupuis. Then we saw you pass through the back lane several times. Don't tell us it wasn't to go see him!"

The boy feels trapped.

"What is the relationship between Paul and Luc?"

"I don't really know Paul. He's just helping Luc with union stuff." The boy feels like the more he tells the truth, the less they will believe him.

"Did you know that Paul Dupuis has a police record?"

"..."

"What else do you know about Paul Dupuis?"

"Nothing. He's just a union leader."

"Why are you defending him?"

"I'm not defending him, I'm telling you what I know."

After two more hours of questioning, Gaétan is taken back to his cell. He walks mechanically, eyes straight ahead, not even trying to get a glimpse at the other prisoners.

He sits down on the side of the bed, completely defeated. He quietly tries to gather his thoughts and realizes that if he isn't released before tomorrow night, he won't be able to get to work on time. He'll lose his job. His mother won't be able to count on his wages to make ends meet. In a burst of energy, he pushes himself up and bangs on the door in a fit of rage.

"Goddammit! Let me out! I didn't do anything!"

"Calm down, kid! We didn't do anything either, and we've been here for two weeks. Get a grip. They'll let us out eventually. Save your energy."

His whole world is falling apart. It's like he's in a car driving a hundred miles an hour towards a wall. He can't control anything anymore. He can see his life slipping through his fingers.

The boy bursts into tears.

Suddenly, he hears the voice of the prisoner in the next cell. He sounds serious. This man could undoubtedly be his father. He listens.

"Keep your head high, my boy. Gotta be patient. This is all just a little bad luck to shake our will. They're betting that we're gonna leave here frightened. Even if you're here for no reason, don't give them the chance to humiliate you. Don't show 'em your weaknesses. Keep it all inside."

A ball of paper lands at his feet. He unfolds it and tries to read the cramped handwriting.

you need to understand
that freedom
is like breathing
it's only natural
you need to understand
that dignity
must overturn laws
when laws are disgraceful
the way is before us
simple as a path

the way is before us
waiting to be taken

And at the very bottom:

you need to understand
that the worst is over
and the best is yet to come

LWM21*

---

* Free translation of a poem by Michel Garneau written while he was in prison.

AGM21
ce qu'il faut comprendre
c'est que la liberté
c'est comme le respir
c'est la moindre des choses
ce qu'il faut comprendre
c'est que la dignité
doit renverser les lois
quand les lois sont indignes
le chemin est devant nous
simple comme un sentier
le chemin est devant nous
il attend qu'on le prenne
ce qu'il faut comprendre c'est que la vraie justice doit abolir les codes

18

Sunday, November 1

It's been forty-eight hours!

The bells in the neighbourhood churches are calling the 11 o'clock mass. Curled up on the narrow iron bed that is fixed to the floor, clutching the ball of paper in his fist, he finally falls asleep.

Two pieces of toast and a cold coffee bring him back to reality. It's a painful return. Gaétan sits motionless on the edge of his bed. He no longer struggles. He waits. He admires the blue sky from his tenth-storey window. It's a shame he can't see the city. From here, he would have quite the view of his neighbourhood.

Suddenly, a guard opens the door. Gaétan didn't hear him coming. The police officers, constantly accompanying the guard, order him to get his things.

"Where are we going?"

"Hurry up!"

They march the length of the corridor in silence. A door opens, another door closes. A shiver runs down Gaétan's back. The hope he had when he was first let out begins to fade. The turnkey's silence bothers him. Not another interrogation! A door opens; another door closes. They stiffly turn down another corridor.

They leave him alone in a small white-walled room. He stands waiting for five, ten, fifteen minutes.

Two other police officers take over without a word. Their disregard for him is unbearable. They lead him from one room to the next without saying a thing.

They are in front of an elevator. They walk in and take it down several floors. The door opens. Gaétan can sense that they are in the basement. They walk through a half-empty parking lot.

Gaétan can hardly breathe. His heart sinks.

They enter another room with a small booth at the far end. He has to give his name and cell number. In exchange, the booth operator hands him a box. The boy opens the lid. Inside are his clothes.

Relief washes over him.

He's free to go!

One of the police officers heads back the way they came without commenting. The other one tells Gaétan to get dressed. He must do it there. Modesty will just have to wait.

"Sign!"

He does, without even taking the time to read the form. The officer accompanies him to a small metal door. He opens it.

The sun burns Gaétan's eyes. The door clicks shut behind him.

He takes a deep breath, a "breath of freedom," as the poet wrote on the piece of paper that Gaétan has carefully slipped into his pocket.

He feels like jumping for joy and shouting.

He walks along Parthenais Street. Passersby walk on as if nothing had happened, without any idea that he has just spent the past forty-eight hours in jail. Life goes on.

He rushes to Louise's apartment.

He bounds up the porch steps two by two. When he opens the door, he is met with the loud sounds of violent rock music. A strange group is gathered in the dining room. Sitting on cushions, they are listening to Jimi Hendrix's *Hey Joe* religiously. Gaétan doesn't see Louise. He crouches down near the guy he recognizes from the other day.

"Have you seen Louise?"

The boy stares back at him blissfully. Gaétan shakes him out of his trance. He eventually puts together a few words.

"I'm not her mother. You wanna puff? It's good stuff!"

Gaétan is exasperated.

"I just want to know if she'll be back soon."

"Lay back, man. It shouldn't be long."

"Do you have anything except air between your ears?"

"Whoa, no need for insults! If you wanna stay straight, it's your business. Louise sure goes out with some real weirdoes," he mumbles, letting himself fall back into the cushions.

Gaétan doesn't answer. He steps over a body or two and opens the door of Louise's room. Two girls are sleeping on the bed, but there's no sign of Louise. The smell of marijuana fills the room. He turns and walks out of the apartment.

He sits on the steps, sulking. He definitely does not like this place.

Suddenly, he can see the large black cape at the corner of Berri. He rushes over to her, forgetting his frustrations.

"What happened to you?"

The boy starts to tell her about his time in Parthenais.

"Wait, you were in jail? You have to tell me about it!"

Gaétan makes a face.

"There are too many people in your bed."

"That's true!" she says, laughing. "We partied pretty late last night."

"They're pretty messed up."

"Let me drop off the milk and the croissants and we can go grab a coffee at the Fontaine à Johannie. Wait for me, I'll be back soon."

Starving, Gaétan devours a hot dog doused in ketchup, just like he likes them, and tells Louise all about his forty-eight hours in jail. The girl listens to him admiringly as she sips her coffee. In her eyes, Gaétan is no longer quite the same boy she met a few days before.

He has become the hero of an exciting story. Gaétan lays it on thick.

When he's done, Louise tells Gaétan that she spent Halloween with his brothers.

"You invited me. We waited for you. Since you weren't coming and Patrick and Richard were jumping all over the place, we left without you. It was amazing. A ton of other kids ended up joining us. We made quite a wacky crew, with all the ghosts, cowboys, Zorros, princesses, and robots. With my black cape and bright red lipstick, I told people I was a vampire. My false teeth were a big hit. Halloween in your neighbourhood is so much fun!"

"It was real nice of you to take them around."

Gaétan grabs her hand and squeezes it. It's soft and warm. Their eyes meet and they hold the gaze for a moment.

Louise brushes his lips with a kiss.

19

Monday, November 2

Gaétan walks down Dorchester. He feels proud and determined.

"Forty-eight hours in there for a kiss isn't too bad," he thinks to himself.

His lips are still burning.

The night before, he had gone back to work to face the relentless rhythm of the machines and the severe gaze of the foreman, who had welcomed him with a warning.

"This is your last chance."

He hadn't taken his eye off him for a moment. But the boy had not been intimidated. He was brimming with new energy, like someone who had passed a test or gotten through a rough couple of months and could never see things the same way again.

At the end of his shift, the foreman told him that if he could keep up that night's pace, he could keep his job.

At this time of morning, Louise is on her way to class. The boy knows that he won't be able to see her today. He has no choice but to go home. But he's not in a hurry to get sucked back into the whirlwind of family life. The only thing that matters is seeing Louise again.

As soon as he had set foot in his house yesterday, after seeing Louise, his mother couldn't stop talking about the girl. She had asked him hardly any questions about his stay at Parthenais. By contrast, she still could not believe that the girl had come and spent Halloween with his brothers, "like a lovely lady." Gaétan feels that this impresses her more than his two days spent in prison. Instead of welcoming him with open arms, she had been hoping that his arrest would teach him a thing or two, complaining about his father's bad influence.

"I'm not raising my boys to end up on welfare or at Parthenais."

And today, the moment Gaétan steps into the kitchen, she's back at it.

"She's pretty smart, that girlfriend of yours," she says, serving him a pancake.

"Ma, let it go. It's not what you think."

"I don't think anything. I'm just observing. Cute and nice, too. She didn't have to take care of your brothers."

"She might be nice, but I don't want my son hanging around those hippies," his father declares as he enters the room.

"Just what I need," the boy mumbles under his breath.

But Gaétan doesn't want to talk about it. He wants to go sleep.

"She's not a hippie. She's studying at Cégep," he can't help retorting, annoyed.

"Exactly. She doesn't come from our world. You might be in for a disappointment."

"Disappointed with what? She's just a friend."

"Your mother told me she lives in a commune. I don't want you goin' back there. I don't want my son hangin' around a bunch of bums who smoke dope and don't work. They're all living off their rich parents. Believe me, they're gonna end up back with mommy and daddy in Outremont in a few years. Bohemian life's easy for them now."

"Just leave me alone!"

Furious, Gaétan gets up and goes into his room. He doesn't want to talk about this. Anyway, it's his business and his father should stay out of it. He works, he's earned his freedom. He can see whomever he wants.

As he slips into bed, he can still hear his father griping. The boy can't help smiling since, after all, he agrees with most of his opinions. Except for one: Louise is different.

Gaétan rummages through a display of LPs. He has come into a music store to look for a gift for Louise. He wants to thank her for taking care of his brothers by giving her a record. It's hard to choose since he knows that she already has so many.

He can at least eliminate the English singers. He doesn't know anything about them, and on principle, he doesn't want to encourage artists that are already playing everywhere. They make enough money, so they don't need his.

His eyes are drawn to a black sleeve with the title written as if it were graffiti scrawled on a wall: *Amour, Anarchie.* He turns the sleeve over and recognizes the singer, Léo Ferré. He's never heard his music, but he's seen one of his albums among Louise's collection. It would be hard to forget this face.

The sales clerk praises the album's music and lyrics, saying that it has just come out. The boy is certain that Louise doesn't own it, but he takes a moment to decide. It's more expensive than the others because it is a double album. Too bad! He can allow himself to splurge on a first gift.

Radiant and proud of himself, Gaétan leaves the store and decides to go drop by Mme Maheu's for a visit.

"Hello! I've got good news for you."

"You haven't come to see me in a while."

"I was pretty busy," the boy replies, not very happy with his lie.

He decided that he wouldn't tell her he was arrested, and especially not that it happened at her son's house. He doesn't want to worry her more. Better to stick to good news.

"A friend told me that under the War Measures Act the police can't hold anyone for more than twenty-one days."

"That means he'll be out soon."

"He should be, unless he's charged."

"Charged with what?"

"Of having ties to the FLQ."

"So it's just a matter of days." After a few moments, she adds, "But this Paul who was living over there, maybe he has ties to the FLQ."

Gaétan thinks that she might be right. Nothing is less certain than Luc's release. Indeed, his apartment had been watched. The police know that Paul had been living there; now he is on the list of suspects. Paul's flight the other night confirmed Gaétan's suspicions that he probably went into hiding for one reason or another. If the police are convinced that Paul is tied to the FLQ, they will definitely charge his friend with helping a terrorist.

But he keeps his thoughts to himself.

"Still, it's strange," she reasons, "that they've kept him for so long. The radio says that they've already released the majority of the people who were arrested on October 16."

"Until they find where they're keeping Cross, I don't think the arrests will stop," the boy tries to reassure her.

20

Tuesday, November 3

Gaétan paces back and forth outside of the college. He's already been waiting for Louise for thirty minutes.

It is cold and grey outside, perfect for snow. But the clouds seem to want to hold back the flakes until the very last moment.

Ten o'clock in the morning. Students are rushing into the large building.

"There's only one missing, and she's the one I'm waiting for," thinks the boy impatiently.

The flood of students turns to a trickle. She still hasn't arrived. He waits for what seems like forever. A wave of fatigue passes over the boy. He hasn't slept at all. His eyelids are heavy.

Suddenly, a hand grabs his own, tugging him towards the Cégep entrance.

"Hurry up, I'm late for class!"

"You told me that you were free."

"My schedule changed. I couldn't let you know. Our literature professor invited a poet to come talk to us about French. I can't miss that."

"Stop pulling me. I can't go to your class with you. We can see each other another day," the boy mumbles, deeply disappointed.

She stops, looking resolved.

"Come on! It's not a problem, our prof is cool, he'll let you in. I'm sure you'll like it. It's Gaston Miron, and he's written such beautiful poems. He was arrested, too."

Gaétan gives in. Because of the girl's sparkling black eyes, her soft hand, the force of her convictions ... and to be with her a while longer.

"Hurry up!"

They fly up the stairs and down a corridor whose magnificent floor creaks under their feet. They pass in front of a series of closed doors; classes have started.

What is he getting himself into? The only thing he knows about poetry are La Fontaine's fables, which he never liked all that much. He fears that the next two hours will be interminable.

The last door of the corridor is the right one.

"It's too late," he tries for the last time. "It's already started."

Without a moment's hesitation, Louise opens the door and pushes him into the classroom.

Thirty pairs of eyes stare at them. Gaétan can feel himself blush all the way to the roots of his hair. Louise drags him to the back row. The speaker seems not to have noticed and continues his speech. He has a loud voice and makes sweeping gestures, completely absorbed in his subject. The man sitting next to him, undoubtedly the professor, nods a welcome to Louise.

Gaétan tries to make himself as small as possible. Being once again behind a desk in a classroom seems strange. He doesn't have such fond memories of school, yet he wasn't a bad student. He did well enough, in fact. But deep down, he had always known that school wasn't for him. So why listen?

However, he finds himself riveted to the man gesticulating in front of him. Behind his horn-rimmed glasses, his gaze is bright and persuasive. To his great surprise, not only is the speech easy to understand, but he is also expressing ideas that seem just and fair.

When Louise spoke about poetry and literature, Gaétan hadn't been so enthralled. But now he feels like this man is expressing something essential. He focuses all of his energy on the words.

"It's true that there is a language problem here in Québec. But it's not the problem that you think. The problem is not in terms of French. The problem is English!

"The problem is that our language is being assimilated by English.

"The language of the French Canadian people is French. It is spoken in variations, sometimes it borrows from English vocabulary, but it is essentially French. *Cheval* or *joual,* it's still French.

"But too often, especially with the elites, our language is a language of translation. And as long as one needs to know English to earn a healthy living, the problem will not be resolved.

"Take, for example, a *pharmacie à prix réduits*. It seems like French, there isn't a word of English, but it's just a calque. It's what I call 'translated from.' The structure is English.

This language is even more dangerous than the one that simply borrows English words.

"To say *pharmacie à prix réduits* is far worse than saying *passe-moi le* wrench.

"There is no more meaning to the language. I could walk into this pharmacy and ask the pharmacist, 'Are you looking to sell your store? I am interested.' What the pharmacist means is that his drugs *sont à vendre à prix réduits,* that they're on sale.

"French appears to remain in this expression. That is alienation. It means you are becoming a stranger to yourself.

"As long as a language evolves on its own, it's fantastic; when it evolves in relation to another, it becomes a passive language. It becomes simply the imitation of the other.

"In Québec, we live in stereo. We always have the translation: *pont*-bridge, pull-*tirer,* welcome-*bienvenue.* We are unilingual bilinguals.

"The French Canadian people speak French. They use English words, of course, but the structure of the language is French.

"Our elites, on the other hand, speak French using an English syntax. I hear it every day. Listen carefully to the ministers and politicians. It seems like French because there isn't a word of English, yet still it's English. We have one language on top of another. By seeing ourselves as others, we become the others. Our language is a dependent language. It evolves in line with the other. The other is embedded in our language.

"Unless you decide to change that.

"So, to restore the French in our speech, we must tear the English out of our mouths.

"Our language must be sovereign.

"So we can return to our roots.

"We can recover.

"We can repossess."

There is a moment of silence. The class is frozen, stunned by the speech. Then, thunderous applause.

Gaétan has tears in his eyes.

He thinks of Mme Maheu.

He finds that being able to put words to suffering already eases the pain. It means that the rebuilding has already begun.

21

Wednesday, November 4

Gaétan slept poorly. He wakes up a bit groggy. What has he been battling in his sleep? He hadn't dreamed; no image comes to mind. But a feeling of powerlessness torments him, like one of those nightmares where you just keep on falling.

He doesn't even feel like getting up to go see Louise. Why should he go see her for a few hours and change the world, only to go back to the factory at night?

How much longer will he keep doing this?

For the first time, he feels as if he's throwing away his life at the factory.

He is beginning to understand his father's rages and his mother's bitterness. He can feel their pain made through disillusionment and surrender. They've gone through the wringer of life.

Today is his birthday. He is sixteen. Perhaps the weight he feels on his shoulders comes from that. He doesn't know if he should be happy or sad. What is the point if he is only going through the motions? He feels as if he is sinking.

He thinks back to the poet who was gesticulating in front of him yesterday, using angry words to express the pain of a people who are dominated even in their own language. It was a man who had chosen to stand up.

A door slams and feet race up the stairs. As always, his two brothers tumble into his room. They scream:

"Happy birthday!"

"Come on! Get up!"

They tickle him. He struggles, but they know all of his sensitive spots too well. He gives it right back to them. All three writhe with laughter.

"Leave me alone if you want me to get up!"

This is all he needs to sweep away his dark thoughts. You shouldn't be too serious when you're sixteen.

His mother and father are waiting for him in the kitchen. A birthday cake sits on the table. He counts: all sixteen candles are there. He blows them out with one breath. His family launches into: "Happy birthday to you, happy birthday to you..."

His brothers hug him. His parents hold him tightly in their arms. They seem happy. Deep down, they are proud of their son who has begun his life as a factory worker.

His mother gives him her gift: a sweater that she has knit for him. His father gives him a hunting jacket.

"We'll get back out there next year."

His two brothers hand him an envelope. Inside he finds a ticket to a Charlebois concert.

"I love you guys! I've been wanting to see him live for so long! Thank you!"

His mother explains that the two boys had saved up their money from the deliveries they make each weekend for the neighbourhood grocer and they had been collecting empty bottles.

Moved, Gaétan doesn't know what to say. In his family they aren't given to sharing their emotions. Feelings are generally kept inside. But being so warmly surrounded is comforting; he realizes that his family is still his best sanctuary.

After supper, everyone gathers around the small screen to watch the show *Moi et l'autre*. They wouldn't miss it for anything in the world. But Gaétan has better things to do; he takes this moment to slip out.

"Where's he goin'?" his father worries.

"He's going to see his girlfriend."

"The one who lives in the commune? It might not last that long. But now that he's working and goin' out and meetin' girls, he won't hang around here too much longer."

"I'd like to keep him a bit more."

"Don't get your hopes up. The bird's gonna leave the nest soon."

"Hey, be quiet! We can't hear Dominique and Denise's jokes."

Gaétan knocks. No answer. He enters. The apartment is dark, but Louise had told him to come by her apartment to celebrate his birthday. He goes as far as the dining room.

Suddenly, rock music bursts from a thousand places and light splashes everywhere, dazzling him. Louise jumps into his arms and kisses him.

"Happy birthday! I made them all leave for tonight. I didn't feel like having them around. Happy to be sixteen?"

"I dunno. I've been all mixed up since this morning."

"You feel sick?"

"No, it's in my head. I don't know what I'm doing anymore."

"Here, I have a present for you."

She hands him a small, flat package. He opens it, touched.

A book.

It's the first time someone's ever given him a book for a present. He's a bit overwhelmed.

"Look at the title and author."

L'Homme rapaillé by Gaston Miron.

"There are some terrific poems in a really distinctive style. His language is sovereign, just like he said. He reinvents the way to talk about love. He expresses the pain and longing of someone who wants to build an entire country."

Swept up in her enthusiasm, she opens the book and begins to read at random. Gaétan isn't used to these words. He doesn't really understand what they mean, but their rhythm and sound are strong enough to blow him away. He could listen to this forever.

Unfortunately, he has to break the spell.

"I have to go. You know, every day I feel less like going to the shop. I'm not lazy, but—it sounds strange to say—I feel like I'm wasting my time, like there's just a dead end ahead. Sometimes I wonder if I should go back to school. Ever since I spent those two days locked up, nothing's the same. I'm all confused and I feel like life is all off track!"

"You know, you can get your diploma by going to night school. And after, at Cégep, you can apply for a scholarship. You'd finish in two years instead of one. It might be worth it to try. I could help you."

"I don't know if I could work and study at the same time."

Gaétan is silent for a moment, thinking. Then, almost sheepishly, he adds, "And I don't really want to leave my neighbourhood. I love it there. It feels alive, all the colours and the smells. I just want the people in my neighbourhood to be respected so they can live properly and earn a living in their own language."

"Maybe you should consider going into politics!"

22

Thursday, November 5

Le Journal de Montréal is lying on the kitchen table. On the front page are pictures of the members of the FLQ who have just been arrested. The headline declares that the police have just broken up an FLQ information cell known as the "Viger Cell." The members are mainly eighteen to twenty-five-year-olds. Among them Gaétan recognizes Paul.

He sinks into his chair.

He was right; Paul has ties to the FLQ.

Gaétan keeps reading. The article explains that for the past few weeks police have been searching for this labourer who has been involved in the trade union struggles. According to them, he went into hiding in early September. He already had a police record and spent several months in jail for planting bombs in Westmount mailboxes. His cell, the Viger Cell, had been created to distribute FLQ reports.

Gaétan thinks about the paper with the *Patriote* header that he saw lying on Luc's kitchen counter. Everything becomes clear; he realizes now that he just missed out on getting caught up in something completely out of his control.

And Luc?

He rereads the article carefully, but his name doesn't appear anywhere.

"Anyway, if all this is true," Gaétan thinks, "they won't release Luc. The police know that Paul slept at his house. He'll probably at least be charged with aiding terrorists. There's definitely a reason he hasn't been released yet. Poor Mme Maheu!"

In a different article, the newspaper also reports that several individuals who were being held since October 16 will appear in court today. But again, there is no mention of Luc.

Gaétan folds the newspaper up and decides to pass by the courthouse to see if his friend is among the accused. But just as he is about to leave, there is a knock at the door.

"Now's not a good time," he grumbles as he goes to answer.

Luc is right there in front of him, beaming. The two friends exchange a warm hug.

"So, we goin' to get that beer? I just got back from some forced time off at Parthenais Beach. I've got so much to tell you."

"Me too. You're just in time, I was about to head to the courthouse. I was sure you were gonna go before the judge today."

"You thought I was in the FLQ?"

"I gotta admit that with everything that's happened in the past three weeks I don't know what to think now!"

"Well I don't know anything. They kept us in solitary confinement the whole time. Zero information from the outside world. You'll have to tell me all about it."

"Look at the newspaper, there's a picture of Paul."

"Why?"

"Read the article."

Luc frowns.

"Unbelievable! That guy can't possibly be a terrorist. He always told me you had to get involved in unions if you wanted change. And he would never hurt anyone."

"Maybe he was sick of being nice. Did you know that he was staying at your place for a few days while you were in jail?"

"That's possible. He told me he'd lost his apartment 'cause he got into a fight with his landlord. He was looking for a place to stay. I told him he could come whenever he wanted. I didn't think it was to hide. But you're right—I got pretty close to being charged. But the police must have believed me because in the end they let me go. Pretty long, three weeks. Anyway, if there's one thing I learned, it's that one day we're gonna get our country back! I don't think they got anywhere by throwing all those people in jail. The opposite, actually."

"I don't know ... Most people support the government, and Mayor Drapeau was re-elected, hands down."

"You got any other good news for me?"

"I think I fell in love."

"Wow! You'll do anything when I'm not around!"

The two friends head out, wrapped up in their winter coats. As the first snow falls lightly over Montréal, they walk with a spring in their step towards the tavern, ready to change the world. And this time, winter has certainly arrived.

Timeline: Québec, October 1970*

October 5: the FLQ's Liberation cell kidnaps James Richard Cross, British Trade Commissioner to Montréal. They issue a statement demanding the release of twenty-three detained FLQ sympathizers as well as the broadcast of the FLQ Manifesto.

October 7: first radio broadcast of the FLQ Manifesto on the CKAC radio station.

October 8: the television news anchorman on Radio-Canada, CBC's French network, reads the FLQ Manifesto.

October 10: Québec's Justice Minister refuses to negotiate with the FLQ. This decision prompts the

* From Louis Fournier's F.L.Q., *Anatomy of an Underground Movement,* NC Press, 1984, and *F.L.Q. Histoire d'un mouvement clandestin,* Lanctôt, 2001.

Chénier cell to kidnap Pierre Laporte, Québec's Deputy Premier and the Minister of Labour.

October 11: Robert Bourassa, Premier of Québec, announces his intention to negotiate with the FLQ. In fact, the supposed negotiations are meant to stall for time.

October 14: "Call of Sixteen." Sixteen eminent Québec personalities, including the head of the Parti Québécois, René Lévesque, the publisher of *Le Devoir,* Claude Ryan, and three union leaders call for the government to release the FLQ sympathizers in exchange for the two hostages. The Call of Sixteen leads to rumours about a provisional government and the threat of a coup.

October 15: the Canadian Army sends 8,000 troops to occupy Québec.

October 16: at 4 o'clock in the morning, the federal government proclaims a state of "apprehended insurrection" and invokes the War Measures Act. The Canadian Bill of Rights is suspended. In the hours and days that follow, some 500 people (actors, singers, poets, writers, journalists, union leaders, and activists) are imprisoned without a warrant. Prisoners could be detained incommunicado for up to twenty-one days without access to their families or a lawyer.

Ninety percent of detainees are released without charge. The army protects rich neighbourhoods and government buildings.

October 17: the Chenier cell announces that Pierre Laporte has been executed. The circumstances of his death remain unclear even today.

October 20: Pierre Laporte's state funeral.

October 25: Montréal's municipal elections are held; Mayor Jean Drapeau is re-elected with an overwhelming majority.

November 5: release of almost all prisoners still being detained since their arrest on October 16. Only twenty-four people are brought to court, the majority of whom are acquitted.

November 6: Bernard Lortie, member of the Chénier cell, is arrested.

November 25: after trailing the suspects, police discover where James Richard Cross is being held in Montréal-North.

December 3: following negotiations with the FLQ, Cross is released after fifty-nine days of captivity. In exchange, his abductors are granted safe passage to Cuba.

December 28: Paul Rose, Jacques Rose, and Francis Simard, all members of the Chénier cell, are arrested.

January 4, 1971: the Canadian Army withdraws its troops from cities in Québec, but the War Measures remain in force until April 30, 1971.

ALSO FROM BARAKA BOOKS – WWW.BARAKABOOKS.COM

YA FICTION

Break Away 1 Jessie on My Mind
Sylvain Hotte (translated by Casey Roberts)

Break Away 2 Power Forward
Sylvain Hotte (translated by Casey Roberts)

The Adventures of Radisson: Hell Never Burns
Martin Fournier (translated by Peter McCambridge)

GENERAL FICTION

Washika
Robert A. Poirier

Principals and Other Schoolyard Bullies, Short Stories
Nick Fonda

I Hate Hockey
François Barcelo (translated by Peter McCambridge)

On the Crow and Other Stories
Robert A. Poirier (November 2013)

NONFICTION

A People's History of Quebec
Jacques Lacoursière & Robin Philpot

Trudeau's Darkest Hour: War Measures in Time of Peace October 1970
Ed. Guy Bouthillier and Édouard Cloutier

The History of Montréal, The Story of a Great North American City
Paul-André Linteau (translated by Peter McCambridge)

Soldiers for Sale, German "Mercenaries" with the British in Canada during the American Revolution (1776-83)
Jean-Pierre Wilhelmy

The Question of Separatism, Quebec and the Struggle over Sovereignty
Jane Jacobs

Parkour and the Art du déplacement
Vincent Thibault (Translated by Casey Roberts)

Roads to Richmond, Portraits of Quebec's Eastern Townships
Nick Fonda